Mouse's Tank
The Legend Retold

Mouse's Tank
The Legend Retold

Mike Donahue

Stephens Press • Las Vegas, Nevada

Editor: Joan Clucas
Cover Illustration: Melissa Rogers
Art Director: Sue Campbell
Designer: Christine Kosmicki

ISBN ISBN-10: 1-932173-55-2
ISBN-13: 9781-932173-550

CIP Data Available

STEPHENS PRESS, LLC
A Stephens Media Group Company

A Stephens Media Group Company
Post Office Box 1600
Las Vegas, NV 89125-1600

www.stephenspress.com

Printed in Hong Kong

For my love, my life, my wife — Linda.

And Garth, always a friend, ever a brother.

Prologue

The Mojave Desert is a hundred thousand square miles of sand, sagebrush and scarceness where life is a strenuous, never-ending struggle. Plants and animals exist in a precarious balance that often depends, day to day, on which way the arid wind alters the immutable face of the desert.

Mile after mile of dry rolling hills blanketed with a sparse, stubbly cover of dusty, pale-green sagebrush cover the Mojave . . . Waxy-leafed creosote bushes that secrete a substance from their roots wards off encroaching members of their own species, and spindly, yellow grasses provide cover for long-legged, black-tailed jackrabbits and ravenous, yellow-eyed coyotes.

Near Las Vegas, Nevada, at the northern tip of the Mojave, Mt. Charleston rises to 11,918 feet of immense, regal splendor. The craggy mountain anchors the desert, keeping it securely fastened against the savage winds that scream down from the heights to flutter the dry expanse at its feet.

Mt. Charleston is a vast natural temple where snow often clings in frigid indifference to the springtime temperatures already warming the desert below. Different elevations are temple rooms encompassing distinct species of animal and plant life.

In one zone of altitude, Joshua trees spread dagger-leafed branches in perpetual wide-armed postures of mute worship. While the green and brown supplicants can appear at many different elevations including the desert floor, on Mt. Charleston they are most readily seen beginning at 3,000 feet. Above 6,500 feet the presence of the obviously hardy trees gradually fades and disappears. Between the two altitudes, Joshuas thrive in a copious but confined forest of life. The trees are seemingly captured forever on the slopes of Mt. Charleston in one thin belt of elevation.

Each spring, flowers bloom on the Joshua trees, colorful offerings of vivid beauty in the Mt. Charleston temple. Yucca Moths swirl among the long, pointy leaves of the trees inspecting the vibrant blossoms like dainty flying flowers tasting the nectar of another. On lacy wings they float from tree to tree in a seemingly random pattern and carry pollen on delicate, tiny legs from one lusty tree to another, fertilizing and spreading life in a carefully choreographed dance in the temple of existence.

Joshua trees do not flourish on Mt. Charleston below 3,000 feet or above 6,500 feet, not because they could not grow lower or higher, but because the Yucca Moths cannot live below 3,000 feet or above 6,500 feet. Continuance of the rugged, hardy tree is dependent upon the small delicate wings of the Yucca Moth. To disrupt the flight of the moth is to disrupt the life of the Joshua. To kill the moth is to kill the tree.

On the broad slopes of Mt. Charleston where the Yucca Moth lives, the story of life for the Southern Paiute tribe of Native Americans begins. From this tall craggy mountain of creation, Southern Paiutes emerged and expanded until they called a vast area in and around the Mojave Desert home, and here they have lived for eons. As with all desert beings, the Paiute life was hard. Food and water were scarce and difficult to come by, but the Southern Paiutes, the People, grew and learned. They settled in river bottoms where the ground was fertile and hunted the many animals that lived in their lands — rabbits, squirrels, even desert bighorn sheep. The Southern Paiutes grew strong from the meat. Fish from the rivers filled drying racks and the exquisite baskets of the People held many natural seeds and grains. The Southern Paiutes found their existence rewarding and worth living to the fullest.

Like the Joshua tree, the Southern Paiutes grew strong and stout and thanked Mt. Charleston and all things for life.

Then the white man discovered and invaded the lands of the Southern Paiutes. He stomped through the desert and stole the land, claiming it for his own. Year by year, step by step, the white man took more and more land, pushing the Southern Paiutes further and further onto sterile and barren reservations.

The white man did not love the land, and ran roughshod over the desert and river bottoms with boots that left hard and relentless footprints. In the dusty footprints of the white man, left as they trampled over the land and the backs of the Southern Paiutes, lay the broken and crushed bodies of delicate moths.

This is the story of one Southern Paiute who saw the bodies and fought to save the moths.

Chapter One

endure — vi **1:** to continue in the same state:
LAST 2: to remain firm under suffering or
misfortune without yielding. vt **1:** to undergo (as a
hardship) esp.   without giving in : **SUFFER 2:**
tolerate, permit

The warm desert sand felt good under Mouse's
bare feet as he walked in the early morning. The fine
grit rubbed between his broad toes, spilling over his
toenails and the tops of his feet. Dust rose with each
step in small cloudy puffs that clung to Mouse's dark
skin giving him grayish socks beneath his brown
trousers. His steps made regular, faint scrunching
sounds in the sand and lizards and small mammals
froze, waiting until he passed.

Grains of the fine sand occasionally stuck between Mouse's toes, but each step pushed it out. Mouse had a pair of white man's shoes slung over one shoulder, the tied laces served as a built-in handle, but it was better in the early summer morning to walk in the warm sand with no shoes, even if it did stick between his toes. The shoes might be needed later, however, so he kept them. They had been given to him by the Mormons in St. Thomas, Nevada.

The Mormons gave Mouse the shoes; the long sleeved, collarless shirt he wore buttoned all the way to the top, and also the brown trousers which covered his legs. He believed the Mormons gave him these things because they wanted him to come to church with them and become a Mormon. In 1896, the Mormons were always trying to get the Southern Paiutes to join their church. Mouse would take everything they wanted to give, but he would never become a Mormon.

He stopped and squinted into the sun over his back-trail. The lines crinkling out from the corners of black eyes deepened as he surveyed the ground. His steps had left hollows in the sand and he could see his track weaving through the pale, pungent sagebrush on the gradual slope behind him. The Mojave Desert air was clear and sharp. Not a cloud showed in the deep blue sky. Mouse knew there would be no wind today to blow dust and cover the regular depressions left by his feet. Even a white man sheriff should be able to follow that track, Mouse thought.

He turned and continued northwest up the slope toward the jagged red peaks in the distance; his steps scrunch, scrunching in a steady cadence. In four hours the fiery summer sun would turn the sand scalding hot and even his heavily calloused feet would feel the heat. Already, larger desert dwellers like the coyote and kit fox had taken shelter. Blistering July days were for resting and sleeping while the cool nights were for hunting and traveling.

Mouse knew this, but he also knew the white man sheriff, John Currie, would be after him this day. Three nights ago he had broken a small window in Bunker's General Store in St. Thomas in order to take a broad-bladed hunting knife and sheath from a front display. It was not the first time he had taken things from the small general store, but it was the first time he had broken a window, and it was the first time someone had seen him.

Mouse saw the woman who witnessed him breaking the window. He knew she raced home and told her husband, who told someone else, who told someone else, until by noon the next day, everyone was aware of the incident. By the following day, Mouse knew the Mormons in the town had gotten word to Sheriff John Currie who spent most of his time in other parts of Southern Nevada. The Mormons had left Mouse alone, knowing that the sheriff would come to St. Thomas this day and he would take care of the Southern Paiute.

Sheriff John Currie would come from wherever he had been and he would arrest Mouse for stealing the knife; arrest him and lock him in jail. Mouse knew this and it was not good. He had been in jail before and he didn't like it.

St. Thomas, where the Muddy and Virgin rivers met before trickling some twenty miles south to add their meager splashes to the Colorado River, had a tiny jail made from quarried stones. There were two windowless cells in the jail and a wooden door that stayed closed until the prisoners were fed twice a day; morning and night. The door had a tiny window with thick iron bars that let in air and enough light during the day so a man could pass the time counting the rocks mortised together in his stone home.

Each cell had a flat place in one corner on which to sleep, a blanket to roll up in and a small metal pot to use as a toilet. The gagging stench that rose from the dirt floor, however, belied the pots.

It was used much more often than the dented metal containers. In summer, the St. Thomas jail was like the vast stone structures built near Ely, Nevada,to make charcoal. Hot enough to make wood smolder, the immense ovens were airless to prevent flames from consuming the wood. Men in the St. Thomas jail smoldered but never burst into flames; not as long as they were inside.

Although Mouse thought it was a foul place, he also knew it was nothing he couldn't stand, as he had already endured it for two days, sitting out a sentence for taking and eating a tomato. But Mouse knew he would be locked up for many days for breaking the window and taking this knife; too many days for a Southern Paiute who loved the freedom of life.

The white man's law seemed a strange thing to Mouse. He had been arrested in St. Thomas for taking food; the tomato. His punishment, decided by the sheriff, was to sit in a place, the jail, where the people who had had him arrested were forced to feed him food the same as that which he had taken.

Mouse said the law made no sense.

"Why has the law not punished the men who stole Southern Paiute land?" he asked Sheriff John Currie. "Should they not be locked up in this small jail to smell the rot of confinement as the stone walls slowly closed around them?"

Mouse said the white man's law was crazy. Like the white man himself, who had no business intruding and interfering into the lives of the Southern Paiutes, or the Nuwuvi, the People, as they call themselves. Sheriff John Currie said Mouse was a rotten renegade redskin who would someday push him too far, and he would lock Mouse up for good; lock him up or kill him.

Stupid white man sheriff would have to catch him first.

Mouse was carrying the knife from Bunker's store in a brown, coarse hemp sack in which he carried all his belongings. The sack had once been used to carry salt from an ancient mine near the Virgin River. As he walked, he hefted the sack with one hand and felt the hardness of the knife through its thick, rough material. He had been looking at the knife in the display case for several days and he had wanted it badly, but it cost $2.50, more than a working month's wages. He hadn't worked in many days, and he didn't plan to. He was glad he had taken this good knife, the best of all the knives displayed in the case.

Mouse reasoned that the whites had stolen the lands of the People, and for this, he would take what he wanted from the whites. He would trade one thing for another, until he was satisfied. It was the way things should be.

As Mouse worked his way up the slope, he stepped on a thorn from a tiny desert cholla cactus. The sharp lance buried itself deep in the skin of his second toe on the tender inner side next to his big toe. Mouse stopped to pull it out. He checked his back trail again then knelt and tugged the thorn from his foot. A small drop of very red blood followed the tiny spear from his toe and Mouse carefully wiped the blood onto an index finger then licked the salty blood from the finger. It was moisture, life in the Mojave Desert. The small clean spot on his foot would last for only one step. Then it would be as before.

Mouse liked to think of himself as a thorn in the toe of the white man. A thorn that could not easily be pulled out and one that would cause much bleeding. If nothing else, Mouse thought that if he could dig deeply enough into the flesh of the white man, they would think twice about taking any more Nuwuvi land.

Mouse had left St. Thomas through the middle of town. He had been carefully obvious and many had seen him leave. At least one would tell John Currie which way he had gone. Again Mouse looked back over his trail. He knew in his mind the sheriff wouldn't be coming for some time, but keeping one eye to his back was a habit of the heart; a good habit for a man like Mouse.

Mouse had heavy black hair that hung down either side of his round face. The strands of his hair were coarse, oily and beautifully shiny. He chopped his hair off square, midway against his strong neck. Sometimes he wore a folded strip of cloth tied around his hair and head. The cloth was red once, but now it was dirty black from the sweat and grime it had absorbed from Mouse's hair and forehead. It was in the hemp sack with the many things Mouse needed to live.

Mouse was a member of the Moapa Band of Southern Paiutes. His people had lived in Southern Nevada for centuries. The People believe their birthplace was on the 11,918-foot Mt. Charleston that rises tall and commanding above the Las Vegas Valley southwest of St. Thomas. Before the whites invaded and stole their land, all of Southern Nevada had been the home of the People. They lived by harvesting wild seeds and grains, growing crops in villages located close to rivers, killing wild game on the desert and catching razor-backed sucker, bonytail chub, and Colorado squawfish in the waters by their homes.

Yearly, Southern Paiutes traveled north to harvest nuts from the dusty, sweet pinion pines that stubbled the northern hills. The nuts were succulent and played an important part in the life of the People.

Mouse was born in 1877 in a small, dome shelter on the newly formed Moapa Indian Reservation on a portion of the Muddy River Valley. The Nuwuvi had been pushed to reservations because the encroaching whites wanted their rich and fruitful homelands on the river bottoms. By the time Mouse was born, some whites were even stealing, planting and running cattle on the little bits of reservation land that held a promise for tomorrow.

He was the sixth child in his family. Only Mouse and one sister survived childhood. Three sisters were killed by measles carried to the Southern Paiutes by Mormon brothers and sisters and one died from the flu in a rugged desert winter.

When his mother had been ready to give birth to Mouse, she sent for help from the other women in the band. Before they could arrive, however, Mouse slipped screaming into the world. His mother told the other women that the boy baby came out so quickly, he was like a little desert mouse scampering from her body. Mouse was never called anything else.

The mahogany skin of his body was darkly rich and smooth with tight, tight pores. He was nineteen years old when he broke the window and stole the knife and although his face had the same smooth skin and tight pores as the rest of his body, it also bore the tiny wrinkles and grooves that would become deep lines and ruts in another 20 years. Just as repeated spring runoffs cut sharp crags and canyons in the barren hills of the Mojave Desert, Mouse's few years had begun to erode the youth from his skin. He bore their passage on his face; at the corners of his eyes and around his mouth.

Mouse's eyes were wide spaced and looked at the world squarely, with truth. His nose was broad and his chin strong. His mouth was a thin-lipped slash across his face that had the curves of a tiny smile built into the slim corners.

He was not a bad man, just a man who believed strongly in his convictions. It also deeply mattered to him that he was a Southern Paiute and that John Currie, who was the law, was white. Mouse had felt the abuse from the whites and he had experienced the degradation they heaped upon the Southern Paiutes even as they stole the People's land. He resented that the whites had taken the land that was once the domain of the Nuwuvi and he had felt the helplessness of being overwhelmed and outnumbered.

But Mouse was also at odds with authority, any authority. Had he lived before the time of the white invasion in Southern Nevada, he would still have had trouble. Had his tribe decided, "This is what is good for us all," Mouse would have questioned, "Yes, but is it good for Mouse?" It was his nature. There have always been such people. Perhaps they make the tribe strong.

He stood and scratched his foot back and forth in the sand. It was warmer now. The rising sun had begun cooking the air, turning it into a thick molten porridge that would cover the desert with a heavy, oppressive heat. Walking, even breathing would become difficult. He took a deep breath and tasted the air. His senses told him it would be very hot and windless today, an uncomfortable day to travel in the desert.

Mouse knew people, mostly white people, had died traveling in the heat of a day like this. There were no springs, no streams in the desert where he was going and with no water, people died. Even the sheriff would know this.

Perhaps John Currie would not come today, Mouse thought. When he arrived in town, perhaps he would tell the Mormons in St. Thomas he had traveled enough for one day and he would chase Mouse tomorrow. It was too hot today to be out running down one Southern Paiute who had stolen a knife.

Mouse looked far behind him at St. Thomas by the river. The tiny buildings in the green oasis of river willows and cottonwood trees wavered and rippled as the bands of heat rising from the desert sand tried to fool his eyes. Mouse looked at the city and in his heart, the heart that always looked over his shoulder, he knew John Currie would not wait until tomorrow. He knew the sheriff would ride into town, check with the Mormons in St. Thomas and then ride out after him.

This is good, Mouse thought. If the white man sheriff waited another day, the trail Mouse had carefully laid down might be blown away and John Currie would not know where to go. This way, he would see his trail and follow it, and Mouse would lead him like he led a horse to water. *Or away from water*, he said to himself and roared with laughter deep inside his chest, although his face never changed and no sound broke from his lips. A desert dweller, he was as frugal with his expression as he was with water. John Currie, would go exactly where Mouse wanted him to go. This was a good thing.

Mouse turned and continued up the slope. He moved not with the exaggerated heel-toe, heel-toe step of the white man, but with the slight heel-toe, side-to-side rocking motion of all Nuwuvi; it keeps them in touch with the powers and rhythms of the earth. In a moment he reached the summit of the ridge that formed the western side of the river valley where St. Thomas stood. Without another backward glance, he quickly crossed over the top, moving from the sight and sphere of the white man, into the domain of Mouse, the Southern Paiute. His steps scrunch, scrunched in the warm sand.

Chapter Two

Mouse squatted in the shade on the smooth rim of a red sandstone ledge forty feet above his trail at the north end of the Muddy Mountains. His toes gripped the sandy ledge and his arms rested easily on his knees. He was the color of the rock on which he sat; invisible to anyone more than twenty feet away. Sitting quietly, he chewed a wad of sticky extract from the root of the gum bush and his jaws were the only part of him that moved. His jaws and his eyes, which scanned the rugged country below for Sheriff John Currie.

One hour before he'd climbed the cliff, some two hours after walking from the valley where the Muddy and Virgin rivers met, Mouse had stripped off his white man shirt and trousers and replaced them with the breechclout he normally wore. This uniform of the Nuwuvi was more practical and comfortable. He placed the shirt and trousers in his gunnysack. Also inside the heavy hemp bag was a pair of Nuwuvi-made sandals for his feet and a hard, pale yellow gourd that held three cups of water; about one fifth the amount most white men would need to drink to survive a summer day in the blistering Mojave Desert.

Mouse took a mouthful, then recapped the gourd and returned it to the sack. He moved the water around in his mouth wetting every tooth, every fold, every pore. The cleansing, cool water was good against his gums and tongue, and as he let it trickle down the back of his throat, the moistness made a smooth channel all the way to his stomach. The drink was an extravagance, but he wasn't worried about water.

As he swallowed, he took his new knife from the sack. He pulled the blade from the scabbard and admired the way the tight, leather handle fit his hand. A very sharp knife such as this had a myriad of uses and would cut many things such as roots and limbs of plants, and the flesh and skin of animals. Mouse knew the brilliant flashes of the shiny metal could be a signal from one hill to another. The knife's heavy handle would not only grind seeds and crack pine nuts, but it felt good in his hand. It was good to have this knife, Mouse thought. It belonged.

After putting the knife back in the scabbard and replacing it in his sack, Mouse moved off his trail and lay on his back in a warm pile of red powdery sand. The sand was like the salt from the Virgin River cave the Nuwuvi had mined for centuries; dry and of very fine granules. As he lay in sand, watching, high above the large dark shapes of turkey vultures soared on three-foot wings arched into characteristic Vs. The wings caught invisible desert currents that propelled the hungry, searching birds into effortless concentrics. The unseen flow carried them over the arid land as they scanned for carrion below. Turkey vultures feed almost exclusively on the putrefying flesh of the dead and sometimes they would soar for days before finding food. They were as much a part of the Mojave Desert as the lizard that scampered from sagebrush to sagebrush; as much a part of the desert as the sagebrush itself.

Mouse began to undulate in the sand in which he lay. He ground his body down into the fine red grit — head, arms, legs, torso. He could feel the sand resist then conform to the shape of his stout body. The warm sand stuck to the moisture in his skin; it stuck to the slick natural oil in his hair, and he slowly began to change from a man into living, moving rock. He felt himself become one with the earth.

Mouse sat up and carefully rubbed the red dust over his front, including the dark lids and long black lashes that protected his eyes. In a moment, the transformation was complete; from a Southern Paiute baked mahogany dark by the desert sun, he had become as a sandstone statue. The darkness of skin and hair were now the warm red of the desert. His dark eyes stared like black flinty rocks from his dusty face. He stood and with a shake, cleaned the excess from his body. After thanking the earth for his new color, Mouse climbed to the ledge where he settled himself to wait and watch.

High on the ledge, he could see miles over the parched land. He felt akin to the turkey vultures soaring high above in purposeful circles. It was a powerful feeling to sit invisible on the ledge and watch the world; to see without being seen, to listen without making a sound. Mouse could sit like this forever. He would not move, he was one with the rock; the red rock that in this place bathed his very being with power.

The whites called this area above St. Thomas "The Valley of Fire." Hundreds of millions of years ago, it was the sandy bottom of a vast inland sea. But as the water receded and dried up, the sea disappeared, and left behind it massive dark gray limestone outcroppings containing the bodies and shells of untold numbers of creatures that had inhabited the sea. Also left were huge sandy dunes colored red by the oxidation of the iron compounds in the land. These red flowing dunes slowly solidified and became brilliant red sandstone cliffs, mesas and buttes.

They climb from the sandy desert floor like vast stone monuments. Some are sharp and ragged, as though the omnipotent artist whose work this was, made fire millennium ago, then froze the keen peaks and spires of the flames to stand in eternal remembrance of passionate beginnings; the heat from the blazing statues captured forever in the fiery colors of the desert. Most of the works appear older, their edges muted and smoothed by the ravages of water, wind and time. Carved by a gentler hand into graceful sweeps and folds, still they smolder with the feverish intensity of creation. Purples, lavenders and a million shades of red and pink splash the blush of life across the face of the natural carvings.

The Valley of Fire was a special, hallowed place to Mouse and the Southern Paiute. All things to the People — rocks, wind, rain, flowers, all things — have the energy of life. In the Valley of Fire the energy of life was very strong. For millennium, it has been a place of awakening for the People, a place of birth.

To the Nuwuvi, this was a place where Mother Earth reached out with massive, straining fingers and touched the wonder of the sky. In this Place of Birth, the earth and sky meld; red below, blue above; the colors of life flow and fuse, mingling to form the marvel of beginning. The Valley of Fire was a living place to the People, where the forces that make all life were strong; strong, and good. In the Place of Birth, there were many powerful sites where the hearts of the People could more easily communicate with the hearts of the others. In the Place of Birth, the ears of the People were opened to the voices of the others; their eyes to the miracle of being.

As Mouse squatted on the red ledge high above his body's signature rubbed into the soft red sand, the music of the Place of Birth played lightly across his skin like a gentle breeze, although there was no breeze. He was one with the rock and he could feel the power and the vastness of the rocks. His senses took in the wonder of the Place of Birth and he knew, suddenly, that Sheriff John Currie finally was coming. Mouse had seen no obvious motion, heard no sound, but he knew in his heart that the white man sheriff was moving across the hot desert into the Valley of Fire.

Mouse's head moved in an imperceptible shake of wonder.

Sheriff John Currie must be very angry to ride his horse out in this heat to chase one Southern Paiute who had broken a window and stolen a knife. He blinked at the intensity of the white man's feeling.

He must be as hot as the yellow sun blazing down, Mouse said to himself. This stupid white man sheriff had better be careful, he could burn up. Sheriff John Currie was starting the chase and it was already 113 degrees in the shade.

Summer in the Mojave Desert is hot. Each morning the rising sun peeks over the horizon and begins heating the dry ground. Despite eight hours of cooling darkness, the rocks and sand retain the warmth from the day before.

As the sun climbs, blinding rays shoot from the sky and fall with blazing intensity onto the face of the desert. Heat swirls across the arid land, melting the coolness in the air. It slowly thickens and, like lava bubbling from an erupting volcano, splashes and covers the ground. It fills every crevice, every wrinkle, every gap with fierce burning energy. In the open air, there is no respite, no place to run.

Some years, it is not unusual for the temperature in the Valley of Fire to crest over 125 degrees.

In the Mojave, the temperature is a tangible force that pushes desert animals deep into dens. Furry coyotes and kit foxes lie in shady darkness and pant away the smothering heat of their bodies.

Desert tortoises scrape and claw methodically, persistently into deep rounded holes away from the life-threatening sun. Even the lizards that leave tiny trails with their tails as they scamper through the soft, red sand become scarce when the temperature passes 110 degrees.

Although Mouse was in the shade, safely hidden from the sun, he could feel the heat swirl across his shoulders and settle across his dark back like a cloak. But Mouse had worn this cloak many times and he was used to its heavy presence. It was part of life in the Mojave Desert.

Drops of moisture squeezed from the tiny pores on Mouse's forehead. Twin rivulets of sweat made thin lines in the red dust on his fine skin from his armpits down his sides to the breechclout that circled his waist. It was nothing. He wasn't worried about water.

Mouse's eyes suddenly narrowed and his breath quickened. Far in the distance, through the wavering heat waves rising off the rocks and sand of the desert, he could see a tiny bay horse carrying the tiny figure of a man. The horse topped a brushy sand dune and stopped. Sheriff John Currie had arrived. The Southern Paiute watched, motionless, as the figure leaned to one side and inspected the ground. Mouse could not see what the rider was looking at, but he knew the trail he had made was singular and easy to follow.

The stupid white man sheriff would think himself a great tracker, Mouse thought. He would think, "Hah. Here is the track of Mouse, the Southern Paiute. I will catch him because he is walking and I am riding on this magnificent bay horse. I will follow his easy trail across the hot desert and catch him by sundown."

Mouse smiled to himself and chewed the gum bush resin. The figure on the horse straightened and Mouse could see the man lift his white hat and rub at the sweat that must be streaming down his face in rivers to soak the shirt below. The rider replaced the hat. From one side of his saddle, he lifted a huge white bag to his face.

This bag contains the water for Sheriff John Currie, Mouse thought. He has brought this much water for himself and his horse and already he is drinking it. It will not be enough. This stupid white man sheriff cannot carry enough water to chase down and catch this Southern Paiute.

The tiny figure on the horse again lifted the white bag to his face, then let it hang off the side of the saddle. Mouse watched as the horse slowly moved down the side of the dune to carry Sheriff John Currie behind a towering red pinnacle into the Valley of Fire. Mouse licked his lips as he thought of the beautiful bay on which the sheriff rode. He had seen this fine, tall horse many times in the stable in St. Thomas and he had lusted after it. Its long black mane and flashing black tail reminded him of the ravishing ebony hair of Nuwuvi women.

The horse was strong, its muscles sleek, smooth and firm. This horse should be his, Mouse thought. What better thorn in the side of Sheriff John Currie than the loss of this horse!

Mouse smiled deep inside, and began to form a plan. This horse would be his horse, and it would be a good thing.

Chapter Three

From the shade behind a tall red spire, a quiet, comfortable Mouse watched a spent white man sheriff strip the saddle and saddle blanket from the back of his exhausted, sweaty horse. The sheriff took the gear from the big bay and threw it in a heap in the dirt at the shadowed base of a large rock in a small sandy clearing on the perimeter of the Valley of Fire. The horse shook its head and its black forelock chased a buzzing fly from its eyes. It nickered softly, gratefully, and Mouse could sense its thirst. For three blistering days, Sheriff John Currie had ridden this horse through the Place of Birth, chasing the dusty footprints created by Mouse's even steps, and the days had taken their toll.

What a magnificent animal, Mouse thought. If I had this horse, Sheriff John Currie could track for a lifetime and he would never come close. It is too bad this horse has to suffer for the actions of this stupid white man.

A healthy horse can drink 30 gallons a day in the sweltering heat of the Mojave Desert and this animal had been forced to share with its rider only the warm three gallons of water contained in the heavy white canvas bag that had been hung from the saddle on its back. It was not nearly enough. The white bag had been emptied at noon when the sheriff and the horse split the last two cups of water.

The sheriff, too, was parched and dry. His shirt and pants were caked with filth where dust had mixed with the sweat that poured from his body daily. His exposed skin bore the ruddy hue of the desert where the fine red grit had filled the lines and grooves in his face and hands. Moving was like rubbing tiny pieces of sandpaper over his flesh; scratchy and uncomfortable. His lips had cracked in the heat and from lack of water. Cracked, too, was the formal veneer he maintained in his official capacity.

Just as Mouse had thought, the sheriff had expected to follow the Southern Paiute into the desert and capture him by evening. The trail was broad, obvious and easy. Sheriff John Currie was smug as he had ridden the bay horse in pursuit of the walking Nuwuvi.

By evening of the first day, however, his smugness had evaporated like a drop of spit in the dry Mojave. The trail seemed to have no rhyme, or reason, or end in sight. It wove through the Valley of Fire like the dusty, patterned back of a desert rattlesnake. It passed over rocky hills, across broad expanses of open desert and it meandered between the high red rock formations of the Valley of Fire in a never-ending plodding. The freshness of the trail hinted Mouse might be just around the next turn, but he was never there, just more footprints.

Sometimes the footprints were of Mouse's bare feet; sometimes they were of his feet clad in sturdy sandals, but Currie recognized the trail both ways.

The second and third days had been more of the same. Mouse's footprints just kept going and going, showing no sign the Southern Paiute ever stopped or took a break from the monotonous trudging that marked his passing. There was no sign Mouse ever took a drink of water, because there was no water the sheriff could see.

By noon of the second day, the sheriff had understood that Mouse, the Southern Paiute wasn't trying to get away, but rather was leading him in a frustrating game of follow the leader. The impatience and rage that began to bubble from under his wide-brimmed straw hat was several hundred degrees hotter than the outside temperature of 116 degrees. From many places along his trail, Mouse had watched the heat grow inside the sheriff. It was as he had expected . . . as he had planned.

Mouse had been very skillful in laying his track. He would walk for a while, then, in a place where a smooth sandstone slab lay next to the path he was making, he would leave the trail and climb up to a high place to check on the sheriff's progress, always being careful to cover any tracks that led off his main course. After seeing where the sheriff was, the Southern Paiute was always careful to go back to the exact place where he had left the trail, and step back onto it, as though it were a continuous line of walking, plodding, escaping. If, after leaving his trail, he discovered the horse and rider were close, the Southern Paiute would veer to a high steep canyon where the going would be rocky and difficult for the horse to pass. If they stopped, Mouse would stop too.

More than once Mouse had been close enough to see the stubble sprouting from the face of the angry sheriff. The gray and dark splotchy spikes on Currie's chin reminded Mouse of a desert thistle. He laughed inside to think of the sheriff's head popping open to release fuzzy seeds that would float on desert currents searching for a place to gain a foothold and grow into a million tiny sheriffs.

For three days Mouse had executed his plan and he knew Sheriff John Currie finally was ready to give up. He had no more water, no more smugness, and no more hope that he would ever catch Mouse as the Southern Paiute was leading him on an extended tour of his desert home. Mouse believed the white man sheriff had learned a lesson. He believed the lawman would leave and not come back.

Sitting quietly, Mouse watched Sheriff John Currie lead his horse to feed on a plot of sparse dry grass. The animal was amazing. It had done everything the sheriff had wanted done with no complaint. It had walked, it had trotted, it had even cantered in the desert heat when the sheriff tried to use speed to surprise his quarry. Mouse felt a great longing for this horse that never complained, never gave up.

The sheriff hobbled the animal then returned to his gear lying in the long shadows of the rocks. He collapsed next to his saddle, leaned his back against the smooth, dark leather and removed his hat. A crown of dirty white circled the sheriff's head where the hat had protected the top from the dirt and burning rays of the sun. His hair lay grimy and greasy against his head.

The sheriff sat motionless, exhausted. He had no more water to drink and he did not eat the meager food he had left in his saddlebags. It was enough for now that he was out of the sun, with or without water. Finally, he was cooling down.

Evening in the desert is a time for renewal. As the sandy expanse swallows the blazing sun, the land takes a deep breath to put out the fire, then exhales in a long cooling sigh. Another moment of burning light would have been too much; but there is never too much. Each day, seconds before the fiery ground would have burst into flames and consumed itself in a crackling, smoke-belching holocaust, the sun disappears and the heat immediately eases. The molten light slowly cools and darkens, and the land begins a refreshing plunge into night.

In the Mojave Desert, evening seems like another dawn. Hungry animals emerge to stretch cramped muscles, and their toothy yawns chase sleep from deep dens. Desert dwellers climb back into the land of the living, and test the cooling air with eager noses and tongues. Revelling in life, small mammals scamper about gathering seeds and other food, while nocturnal predators prepare for the hunt.

"It has been a long day, has it not Sheriff John Currie?" Mouse said in his deep voice. He spoke gently, but the words rode the still, cool waves of the evening and reached the ears of the sheriff as if Mouse were standing over his shoulder.

The sheriff was startled and jumped rapidly to his feet as though he might catch the words if he hurried and followed them to the man who had called out. John Currie glanced quickly around to discover the source of the voice. The dense grayness of the evening, however, distorted his sight, and the reflecting rocks gave the voice an multi-directional quality. Had the sheriff dipped his knees slightly, cocked his head at the right angle and looked for a man covered in the red dust of the Mojave Desert, he might have seen a faint outline of Mouse. But the sheriff was looking for a Southern Paiute with black hair and flinty black eyes; his sun-darkened skin contrasting sharply against a white collarless shirt and strong white teeth. The person the sheriff was seeking, the man who had walked from St. Thomas dressed in brown cotton trousers of the white man, had disappeared the first day of the chase.

"Mouse, is that you? Damn you, get your butt over here," the sheriff called looking wildly about. His voice cracked against the dryness in his throat. "I don't know what kind of game you think you're playing, but this is the end of it. I want you down here right now. You're in a world of trouble."

Mouse sat without moving, without speaking, watching the sheriff. In a few moments the angry lawman kicked at the desert sand, then plopped back down next to his saddle.

"This man is not in the world of trouble," Mouse finally replied. "This man is in the world of the Nuwuvi, his home, just as you are Sheriff John Currie."

Again the sheriff jumped, startled by the voice that seemed to come from inside the rocks around the clearing.

"You know what I mean, Mouse," the sheriff said, this time staying down in the sand. "Don't play the stupid Indian with me."

Mouse sat silently. The cool of the evening played gently over his skin and the desert birds provided a pleasing music.

"I am not the stupid Indian," he said. "I am Mouse the Southern Paiute. I talk the white man's tongue. I can speak with the Shoshone and with the child-stealer Utes. I can talk with the animals, the plants, the wind, all things here in this place. Can a stupid man speak these languages? Can you talk to me in my tongue? Here in my home, can you talk the language of the Southern Paiute? I think that here in this place it is you who are the stupid one, Sheriff John Currie."

"I'm going to get you Mouse," the sheriff said. "I'm going to get you and make you pay for leading me all over this hell-on-earth." The sheriff's once-white forehead was red with the rage that boiled inside.

"Why have you followed me for three days Sheriff John Currie?"

"You know damn well why I've followed you. You're a Goddamn thieving red renegade devil. You broke that window in Bunker's store and stole that knife. You're going to do some hard time for that Mouse. For stealing that knife and making me chase you all over this Godforsaken country you're going to do some real hard time. You come down here now, give yourself up to me, and it'll go a lot easier for you."

"Does this white man say it is wrong to take the property of another?" Mouse asked. His questioning voice sounded sincere, innocent.

"You know it was wrong Mouse."

"Are there white man laws against taking the property of another?"

"Goddamn you Mouse, get your butt down here. Now! I am getting real tired of this." The sheriff was on his feet again, walking from one side of the sandy clearing to the other. He peered into the dark crevasses between the hot red rocks looking for some sign of Mouse.

In the distance a coyote challenged the anger of the sheriff, yipping out its pleasure at life. The silence of the evening grew and the night began to take over. The sheriff sat again and Mouse's voice echoed from the darkness.

"There is a tall tree next to the river where the white man has built the place he calls St. Thomas," Mouse said. "It is the tallest tree in the land. From the top of this tall tree, it is possible to see many miles, although it is not so tall that the People could see what the coming of the white man really meant.

"When this man was a small boy, he would hear the elders talk of playing in the branches of this tree. They would climb up the branches of this very tall tree and from the top survey the world that once belonged to all the People. The land of the People was rich and fertile and from the top of the tree it seemed to go on forever.

"When the day was very hot, much like today before the sand swallowed the yellow sun, the tree would invite all the People to sit and share the coolness under its branches. The breeze would blow and make pleasing music with the leaves of the tree. The tree and the breeze would invite the People to sit and listen to the music of the leaves, drink cool water and talk of life. It was good to do these things. It brought the People together.

"Some years, the tree would take the life-giving sap from one of its many fat branches. Soon, the branch would die and fall. The old ones in the villages of the People would then take this branch and burn it to cook their food or warm their homes. It was good of the tree to do this. It is a good tree.

"The white man says it is wrong to take the property of another, but it is not wrong to give something in exchange for the property. In exchange for this knife that I have taken, I will give you the use of the tall tree of which I have spoken. Talk to it. A smart white man like you can surely talk to the trees.

"Talk to this tree and it will give you shade in the summer. This winter, when you are cold, the tree will give you one of its many fat branches to burn."

"You silly bastard ," the sheriff screamed, enraged. "You think you can come into one of my towns and just take what you want?"

"No Sheriff John Currie. That is what the white man does. The white man goes to places that are not his and says, 'I like this place. I will take it for my own.' It is the white man, not the Nuwuvi who do these things. I have said I will trade you the use of the tree for the use of this fine knife. That is a fair trade. It is a good thing."

"Goddamn it I already own the Goddamn tree. It's in my town."

"Your town is on the People's land. The land where the People for all time have lived and grown grains and squash and many other things."

"This is pointless bullshit," the sheriff said. "Your people were moved to the reservation a long time ago Mouse. You gave up your right to the land years ago. Get your butt down here."

"This man will never give up his right to live anywhere in the land of the People," Mouse replied. "It is time for you to leave this place Sheriff John Currie. I brought you here, to my home, to show you that you do not belong here. It is too late for the river, but it is not too late for the Place of Birth. This land is the People's land. It is a sacred place. Too hot for white men; too hard; too pure. There is no water here for the soft white man. It is time for you to leave."

"Goddamn it get down here," the sheriff screamed. "You have no more rights, no more land; only the reservation. Now get down here. You broke the law. You hear me? You broke the Goddamn law!"

Mouse sat without speaking, listening to the quiet coolness of the desert. A myriad of odors drifted across the sand, over the rocks, splashing and mixing into the scents of evening; a light wafting tea made from the dusty aromas of creosote and sage. The delicate tea soothed the raspy harshness of the Mojave Desert. Gently, like a vast gossamer butterfly wing floating easily over the land, darkness settled and overwhelmed the fiery rocks in the Place of Birth. The colors slowly cooled and faded into the uncompromising black and white of night.

Mouse inhaled and enjoyed the scents of the desert. He spoke no more.

Chapter Four

The scrunching of the sheriff's boots in the sand of the desert clearing woke Mouse before dawn of the fourth day. He had slept comfortably, easily throughout the calm night in a small alcove carved in the sandstone by eons of wind and rain. The bottom of the tight niche was filled with smooth, powdery sand that made a downy red bed.

The sheriff had not taken three steps in the early morning before Mouse was alert, listening. He eased out of the hole in the soft rock and peered over a protecting boulder. Although it was still dark, the area was dimly lighted by the stars and Mouse watched the black shape of the sheriff move to one side of the clearing. Loudly the lawman cursed the lack of water as feeble drops of urine splashed briefly into the sand.

The sheriff moved back to his gear and dropped beside it. Mouse could hear John Currie's probing hand pull dried food from the bags tied to the rear of his saddle. A large whiteness flashed in the dark and Mouse knew the sheriff was shaking his water bag. He heard the sheriff suck at the dryness in the container. There was no more water for the sheriff. It was time for him to leave.

"Mouse if you're out there, I'm giving you one last chance to come on in. You hear me? Mouse? You there?"

Mouse knew the sheriff expected no answer. He was merely yelling out his anger, his frustration. It made Mouse comfortable to know the lawman, like any other creature, was predictable.

"Goddamn you Mouse, you son of a bitch, I know you're out there. I know you can hear me. Get down here. Tell me where you're getting the water that's keeping you going. You got caches hidden around this Goddamn place?"

Only the approaching dawn broke the stillness of the night. Slowly, slowly the heavy, soft curtain that made the darkness was pulling from the eastern sky. Awakening birds chirped out greetings. Scampering lizards quickly entered the daily race for life, ever eager snouts sporting perpetual reptile smiles. Desert insects hummed and the sluggish Mojave awoke.

Mouse heard the sheriff sigh heavily as he climbed slowly to his feet. The nearby horse, which had slept with his legs splayed as far as the hobbles would allow, heard also. He blew and nickered wearily, deep in his chest. Mouse knew the animal must have water soon or it would die. Another day in the blazing desert would suck the life from the horse the way the heat sucked the moisture from all things

in the Mojave. The Southern Paiute, in his mind only, sung softly to
the animal, explaining his actions. Mouse's chant told the bay its
duty was nearly finished; water was only a short time, a short walk
away.

It had been an exhausting night for the horse, but not entirely
fruitless. During the coolness, Mouse had walked on feet of air
and approached the big bay. He had sung softly to the animal and
his voice held meaning and promise for the horse. It seemed to
remember the scent of this Southern Paiute and its voice rumbled
gently.

Mouse had run loving hands over the head and neck of the horse.
He had breathed softly into the wide, sucking nostrils of the horse
and in turn, had inhaled the dry breath from the great brown animal.
Into his cupped hand he had poured water from his gourd and the
grateful horse had sucked at the meager fluid. It was not enough,
but the horse would forever remember the scent and the kindness of
the Nuwuvi man who had eased its pain in the desert.

Mouse would have led the horse away from Currie but he knew
the white man would die if he did. He did not want to kill this stupid
white man sheriff, merely teach him a lesson.

Mouse had a plan for this horse and he could wait. Desert hunters
learn early in life to have patience." Soon," Mouse told the horse.
"Soon you will have water and it will ease your thirst. Carry this
stupid white man back to St. Thomas, back to an easier place, then
this man will come for you." With a final pat, Mouse had slipped
away knowing it would be a long night for the horse and for the
thirsty sheriff as well.

That morning, Currie trudged through the soft clinging sand and
approached the bay. He removed the ropes that had kept the animal
from walking alone the twelve miles back to St. Thomas and cooling
water. He led the horse back to his gear to ready him for the ride

back to town. The big bay was totally spent. He walked listlessly, his head hanging just above the ground. Each step was an effort.

Currie pulled a brush from his saddlebags and purposefully whisked the sand and grit from the bay's fine summer coat. There had been no wind and the horse had been unable to lie down because of the hobbles, but he had somehow managed to pick up a full load of dirt.

"This isn't the end of it Mouse," the sheriff called over the regular cadence of the sweeping brush. It made a whisking sound in the still dawn. "One way or another I'm going to get you. You better be looking over your shoulder every second, because you'll never know when I might turn up. We both know you can't stay out here forever — with no water. You're going to come out this hell hole sometime. Maybe you're going to visit the reservation. Or head into St. Thomas for something. When you do, I'm going to get you."

Mouse listened to the whisking of the brush without speaking. Suddenly, a large hungry chuckwalla lizard ran across the top of the rock near his still form. Fast as a striking snake and with thoughts only of food, the Southern Paiute's hand blazed out and grabbed the fat reptile. Mouse was successful in catching breakfast, but the rasp of the movement echoed through the rocks like a signal pointing toward the hungry Indian. The sheriff spun away from the bay to scrutinize the surrounding rocks. He dropped the horse brush and quickly pulled his pistol from the holster strapped high on his hip. His eyes darted from boulder to boulder. He spun full circle looking for the source of the sound. He knew it was Mouse.

The sheriff leveled his pistol at a dark crevice in the rocks in front and to Mouse's right and with no warning fired a booming shot. The bay horse reared to the length of its lead rope and screamed in fear as the reverberations from the unexpected shot bounced and rattled among the rocks. The whining bullet skipped across the rocks in a deadly random pattern that missed Mouse by inches only. As fast as he could, the sheriff turned left to another shadowed area in the rocks and again pulled the trigger.

The revolver thundered and the bullet carved a deep groove in the red sandstone. The heavy smack of the ricocheting bullet against another rock was lethal and dense. The sound rolled on and desert creatures froze in terror.

Had the sheriff turned right instead of left, he might have seen Mouse pull down behind the red rock, his eyes wide with stunned silence. Mouse was lucky.

Another shot thundered in the clearing and the whine of the ricochet screamed away in the dawn. The booms of the pistol were terrifying. This white man sheriff surely has lost his mind, Mouse thought as he dropped behind the large boulder on which he had been sitting. The lizard he had caught scampered free. This gun he is shooting could kill me. Another shot hammered out and Mouse hugged the warm rock. His heart was beating hard. He could feel every grain of sand beneath his body as he pressed himself into the stone. This crazy man is trying to kill me. The explosive blasts from the pistol had frightened away the fun.

"Goddamn you, you stinking son of a bitch Mouse, I'm going to get you," Currie screamed. "You're going to pay. For the knife, for the three days you have been leading me through this Goddamn waterless place."

The sheriff turned in another complete circle. He was panting with a scalding anger that flooded out in white-hot waves. He shook his head at the madness, frustration and thirst that had shriveled his self control. He fired again and then again. His finger continued to pull the trigger and the hammer of the revolver snapped, snapped on empty rounds in the cylinder. As quickly as it started, it was over. There was quiet in the clearing. The loudest sound in the rocks was the incessant humming of thirsty insects that had ignored the booming gun the way they ignored everything over which they had no control. Mouse heard Currie take a deep shuddering breath.

The sheriff took off his hat with the hand that held the lead rope to the horse. He stood for a moment with his head bowed and his arms hanging limply at his sides — as though praying. He shook his head and took another deep breath. He replaced his pistol in his holster and his hat on his head.

Although Mouse could not see the sheriff, he could hear these things. The sounds indicated this was the time to move. Quietly, he pried his body from the huge rock he had been hugging. His hands and the middle of his chest left dark, wet spots on the stone where nervousness and fear of death had seeped from his body. He crept slowly, noiselessly from his hiding place. His bare feet made no sound in the sand. The skin on his back crawled with a life of its own, fearing the potential burning thud of a bullet.

In a moment Mouse had put several layers of protecting boulders between himself and the clearing where Currie stood with his horse and the deadly pistol. The Southern Paiute checked his back trail and felt surprise at the track that led through the dirt to the bottoms of his calloused feet. In his haste he had forgotten.

Mouse knew the sheriff was retreating, but the Southern Paiute decided to leave nothing to chance. Immediately he backtracked a short distance carefully wiping out his trail. He walked his steps to lead into the mouth of a blind canyon and then crossed over the tops of dry, sandless rocks back to his original trail. He climbed the face of a small cliff and pushed his body into a cramped niche under a red slab to wait. Patience was one of the keys to survival in the Mojave — especially when a crazy white man sheriff was hot enough to kill a Southern Paiute who had only taken a knife, Mouse thought. It was early, but high above turkey vultures soared on invisible currents.

Ten minutes later Mouse heard the clop of a steel shoe against the rock. He turned his head slowly, gently in his hiding place and watched Sheriff John Currie ride his horse between two vast upright stone sentinels to the top of a small knoll thirty yards away. The sheriff turned in the saddle and surveyed the clearing where he had spent the night. In a moment, with a slight tightening of his knees he urged the bay into a walk. The horse trudged laboriously through the sand that sucked at his delicate feet. Mouse admired the heart and stamina of the big animal. It sent a thrill through his body to see that the bay would obey the rider even to his own death. One day, I will have this horse, he thought to himself.

Mouse watched the horse and rider for thirty minutes, until he was sure the sheriff was leaving, then he climbed down from his hiding place. The sun was up and already heating the day.

From the bottom of the cliff Mouse turned south and began to move purposely through the Place of Birth. He frequently checked his trail and at one point climbed a high swirling spire to survey the entire area. There was no sign of Currie.

Forty-five minutes later Mouse dug into the warm sand with calloused hands at the base of a large rock, and remembered the loud, lethal smacks of Currie's bullets. It was good to be able to feel the sand; smell the warmth of the air bouncing from the rocks in the Place of Birth.

In a moment Mouse pulled his gunny sack from its red nest. He shook the dirt from the heavy cloth then pulled out his knife. It was still shiny and warm in his grasp. In the yellow water gourd hanging from around Mouse's neck by a cord, there were perhaps four ounces of water. One slow sip at a time, Mouse drained it. The familiar tepid wetness washed away the bitter tang of fear and Mouse regained his assurance.

Squatting in the sand with his back against a rock, Mouse held his heavy knife and thought of John Currie. He had hated the death carried in the loud pistol, but it had pleased the Southern Paiute to see Currie steam and boil with the rage of impotence. Mouse had known the sheriff would pursue him and it had always been his plan to lead the lawman on a wild goose chase through the Place of Birth.

It was good to have fun in the midst of life as well as show the sheriff he was an unwanted foreigner in this place — in all the land of the People. That this white man would be so angry as to try to kill, gave Mouse second thoughts. He was a Southern Paiute and had known for his all of his short life that death was forever.

Mouse took a moment to look at the things that were his life in the Place of Birth. His dark eyes caressed the hardy sage, the fragrant creosote, the flashy green of the screw bean mesquite trees contrasting sharply with the rich colors of the earth and the clear blue brilliance of the sky. The sights, the sounds, the smells, all things in this sacred place were Mouse's life. Mouse knew this and it filled his heart with an overwhelming joy and reverence for existence; feelings that those who live close to the ground most clearly understand and appreciate.

It was 98 degrees at the base of the rock where the Southern Paiute squatted. The heat this day would hit 119. Mouse reveled that he was here, alive, squatting in the sand, so he could feel it.

After filling the hole and smoothing the sand where his belongings had been buried, Mouse stood. He turned from the rock and walked down a narrow red canyon directly opposite the route Sheriff John Currie had taken back to town. Mouse was home, finally alone, and it was time to move, to get comfortable. His steps scrunched, scrunched in the sand as he made his way back into the depths of the Place of Birth. It was good to be alive and his mind soared. But as his thoughts climbed to float free on rising desert currents, a long wavering black tendril of desire kept Mouse securely tethered to earth.

The tendril was Sheriff John Currie's horse. Mouse wanted this animal as he had wanted nothing else in life. The animal called to him and pulled at his heart. Mouse knew that sooner or later he must have the horse, just as he had to have the knife. And because of his desire, he knew he had not seen the last of Sheriff John Currie; nor of his deadly booming pistol.

Chapter Five

Mouse had been walking through the Place of Birth

for two hours when he turned down a narrow canyon

with a smooth, sandy floor. His movements were not

the steady, methodical plodding with which he had

led Sheriff John Currie, but the quick purposeful

movements of a desert hunter with a planned

destination. Mouse's mouth was open in a slight pant

from the heat. A trickle of sweat seeped from under

the once-red cloth he had tied around his forehead.

The sweat ran down one side of his dark face leaving

a darker streak on his skin. He was quickly losing

moisture from his mouth and his pores, but he was not worried.

Mouse picked up a thick swatch of sagebrush just inside the canyon mouth and carefully brushed away all evidence of his passing in the fine, red sand. To the unknowing, it was as other sites in the Place of Birth — nondescript in its overwhelming magnificence. The many-hued red sandstone spires, cliffs and boulders that made the walls looked no different than those of the hundreds of other tight gorges in the Valley of Fire. Desert varnish, a hard, painted sheen, where moisture, iron and manganese had leached from the rock, lay flat and black on faces of many of the boulders.

Niches, holes and lazy sweeping contours had been carved in some of the rocks by eons of sandy winds that funneled through the canyon like a sculptor's tool. It was an oven between the high swells that formed the walls.

Streaks in the sand on the bottom of this place revealed where lizards had braved the open ground in search of food. The lines where the reptiles had pulled long, useless tails were bordered by tiny evenly spaced footprints. They ran from one spindly bush to another. As Mouse covered his track with a light swish, swish from the sagebrush, he was careful to leave complete trails of the lizards. If he interrupted a mark, he was painstaking in the effort to brush it all out. Half a lizard trail was like an arrow pointing to the passing of a stranger.

Mouse carefully moved down the canyon, swish, swishing with his ragged broom until thirty feet inside he left the sandy bottom and climbed across rocks that would hide his passing. He stored his sagebrush broom in a shallow crevasse. When he left he would reuse the sagebrush broom to again hide his passing.

Mouse slowed as he moved into this familiar place. Though his senses remained alert, the muscles across his shoulders and the back of his neck relaxed. A canyon wren called a shrill warning as he passed below a mesquite tree growing precariously on the steep canyon wall. The Southern Paiute knew a chick-filled nest was firmly woven into a shaggy crook of the tree. He smiled in his heart. This bird would call a warning if any foreigner should pass this way. Mouse thanked the bird for its diligence. It was a good thing .

Mouse missed nothing as he moved quickly down the canyon. The lines deepened at the corners of his dark eyes and he saw every scratch, every twig, every yellow stalk of the tall dry grass that rose from the ground in isolated clumps. None could have entered here without Mouse seeing — sensing — some evidence of their passing. He was satisfied that none had. It was just as he had left it two nights prior when he had raced to and away from this place as Sheriff John Currie slept.

Some three-hundred feet inside the canyon, Mouse could no longer climb from boulder to boulder and he was forced to move back to the bottom of the gorge. There was another sage broom hidden there and again he covered all signs of his passing. He walked and swished with his broom along a meandering river of sand that ran down the center of the canyon. The sand was warm and deep. It sucked at his feet as he walked, slowing his passage through this beautiful place. Green lichen grew on the north faces of huge granite boulders that lay in the canyon. The green, brown, and gray of the lichen created an exquisite and unmatchable pattern of nature. He was glad to be here, experiencing the splendor of life in this place.

Abruptly, after another 50 feet, the sides of the gorge fell away and the Southern Paiute entered a large, rocky, bowl-shaped clearing. Standing on a wide flat rock, Mouse paused.

The day was dead calm and hot. The dazzling sun bounced and ricocheted through the canyon in pinpoints of light that seared into the very consciousness of his being. It was 106 in the open desert, but here, in the bottom of this clearing, where the red rocks gathered the heat and reflected it like mirrors to sizzle the very air, it was 117. Today, at its hottest, the temperature in this canyon clearing would hit 129 and the air would crackle and threaten to turn black as flesh in a fire — but it would not.

Mouse's eyes surveyed the area in minute detail, checking shadows, colors and the tiny motionless pale green leaves on the stunted sagebrush. His eyes swept the canyon walls from right to left. He saw flies clinging torpidly to the underside of a red ledge as they waited out the blistering sun. He could smell the dry ripples of the air as the heat rose in sheets from the red rocks. It was so quiet here the cadence of Mouse's heart echoed in his ears. After checking the stream of sand in front of him, Mouse's gaze swung to the left and came to rest on a vast out-thrust portion of the canyon wall. Millennium ago, a large piece of the wall had sheared off. It lay as shattered rubble at the base of the wall, large stones partially buried in the red sand.

The enormous flat surface of the rock that remained, twenty feet high and forty long, was black with desert varnish. Thin cracks criss-crossed the face of the well-weathered stone the way lines seamed and rippled across the faces of the Nuwuvi old ones. And just as the elderly carried the history of the People in tales filled with word pictures that were carefully and finely drawn with the tools of memory, the pictorial story of life was carried by this rock in carefully and painstakingly etched petroglyphs.

One of many sacred sites of consciousness in the Valley of Fire, the rock was an easel upon which the People, and those before the People, had chipped and scratched the story of life in the dark veneer of the rock. Stories of what had been, what was now and what would come to pass, were chipped in minute detail here in this rock. It was one of many holy spaces throughout this canyon and other canyons in the Place of Birth.

There were beings represented here; desert bighorn sheep, tortoises, humans, and insects. Symbols that carried both the meanings of what they appeared to be, such as crosses, wavy lines, spirals, and what they represented on another, higher plane were depicted as well. The pictures were the art of the people of the Mojave, carved, etched and scraped, one scratch after another. Each tiny chip was hammered out of the dark desert varnish with a hand-size rock to reveal the pale under stone. It took thousands of tedious chips to make a petroglyph.

These petroglyphs were the soul of the People. They expressed the visions of the Nuwuvi — the existence, the meaning and the direction of life, the purpose of being. Many could read this art and discern the flow of life, charting a proper course for a proper outcome. But not Mouse. While Mouse could appreciate the art and labor of art, he had never been able to read the deeper meaning of the petroglyphs.

He had tried many times in the past to understand, to see the true significance. But even after fasting for three days — fasting and dancing to exhaustion in the circle dance of remembrance, the ground pounded smooth and hard under his blistered feet — the other meanings of the pictures chipped into the rock were beyond his grasp. To Mouse the petroglyphs were just images that meant only what they pictured. That he could not read the petroglyphs was as frustrating as the hopelessness he felt about the invading white man.

Mouse was not alone. Not all Southern Paiutes could understand the petroglyphs. For them there were shamen who could read the art as a book and interpret what was there. This was an accepted practice. For Mouse, however, being unable to decipher the pictures was maddening.

He had always reasoned that as a true man of the Nuwuvi, he should be able to understand, but what quirk of fate or dark entity kept him blinded he did not know. An elder of his band once told him his time, his understanding, would come. But Mouse was impatient; much as a hungry young coyote was impatient as it hunched beside a mouse hole; the gnaw in its belly a constant drive that must be acknowledged.

He took a deep breath. Perhaps he would dance again soon and this time understanding would come. It would be good to know if the events with Sheriff John Currie were written in this rock art.

Mouse took one last look around the clearing. The sweat poured from his body just as the Muddy River poured from the earth. It was good to sweat this way — when one was not worried about water. It was cleansing. Mouse nodded to himself then crossed the clearing and re-entered the narrow canyon on the other side being careful to swish away any footprints in the soft red sand.

As Mouse continued down the canyon, he passed other areas where petroglyphs had been made. Some were fifteen feet or more up the sides of the vertical rock faces. The People who carved these pictures had done so at eye level, but water and wind had so eroded the canyon bed that the art was left as hanging oils in a museum.

A quarter of a mile past the entrance where Mouse had come into the slender red canyon, it split in two. The right fork continued for another thirty feet before it slowly closed and finally was blocked by a twenty-ton boulder that had dropped from some lofty perch eons ago.

The left fork of the canyon opened immediately into a brief sandy clearing that continued for some twenty feet. On the right as Mouse entered the clearing was a shear rock face that rose sixty feet straight up. There were no petroglyphs here to mark this place. To the left, a clump of huge rounded boulders channeled the canyon into a steep narrow slit that went nowhere.

Straight ahead were two large boulders that blocked passage. The canyon was closed, there was nowhere else to go.

Mouse walked to the center of the clearing inspecting every inch for any unusual sign. Seeing none he stripped his gunnysack from where it hung around his neck by a thick braided leather cord and dropped it on the ground. The sand here was a different color than that in the other parts of the canyon. A dirty pinkish white, it was littered with many twigs and the stalks of tall dead grass. Mouse could see between the two large boulders blocking the end of the canyon that he was standing on a small cliff.

He knelt and quickly rummaged through his sack to pull out his empty water gourd. With his other hand he dragged a long length of braided cord from the sack and this he tied securely around the neck of the gourd.

Looking at the clearing from the entrance, one could see nothing unusual about this place. It looked like a small box canyon that ended here — a good place to turn around and search for easier passage. Even standing near enough to see into the distance between the boulders, revealed nothing out of the ordinary. But Mouse knew better.

After tying the rope tightly to the gourd, the Southern Paiute approached the huge stones at the clearing's end. From their base, Mouse could see he was not on the rim of the cliff at all; that just beyond and below the spot where the two boulders lay one against the other, there was another vast rock propped vertically against them. In the juncture where the three leaned unyieldingly against one another, there was a deep natural stone pocket, a tank.

Mouse braced himself and leaned out so he could look down into the tank. There, four feet below the lip, the man of the People could see the shimmering, glittering face of life in the Mojave Desert. The tank was two thirds full of water, the precious, life-giving fluid. Holding tightly onto one end of the cord to which his gourd was tied, he dropped the canteen into the tank and listened as it splashed thirstily into the yellowish pool. It floated for a moment then, as the water poured into it, it slowly filled and sank.

Leaning over the tank, Mouse could smell the water; an intoxicating aroma that filled his mind with promise for another day. In the dry air, the humidity rose from the deep basin in waves. Mouse pulled the gourd from the tank and took a long drink at its throat. The water was stale and brackish but nothing had ever tasted better. It was familiar, soothing, life-giving water.

Mouse was home, and the reality of it sent a shiver of delight rippling down his spine. He took the knife from the gunnysack and poured an extravagant trickle of water down its sharp blade. The water ran down the blade and splashed onto the ground, making a dark freckle pattern in the sand. He held the knife high above his head and allowed the sun to caress its steel length. It glinted in the light and rays reflected from the blade and glimmered against the walls of the clearing.

The shimmering, wet flash meant victory — victory over Sheriff John Currie. Mouse savored the moment and shook his fist clenched tightly around the hilt of the knife. From his mouth, in a low voice, he sang to the knife and thanked it for being. Today Mouse had won and exhilaration filled his heart. Today life was excellent.

Chapter Six

Mouse stretched his length as far as he could; tightening then slackening sleep-cramped muscles. He curled his callused hands into tight fists and took a firm grip on the new day before relaxing and listening to the sounds of the awakening world. In the east, directly outside the entrance of the small cave in which he slept, a hint of fire lighted the morning sky. To the west, behind Mouse's cave, he knew the sky was still dark though he could not see the west. Awakening today was a languorous process that would be enjoyed. The dark red sand on the bottom of the cave was feathery, smooth and thick. It was a bed like no other and Mouse lost himself completely in the land of dreams when he lay upon it.

Mouse's tiny cave was 100 feet back up the canyon from the fork that split the gorge in front of the natural water tank. Halfway up on the side of the canyon, it could only be seen by someone who climbed the steep rocky slope and stood directly in front of it on the small ledge that was Mouse's living space.

The Southern Paiute lived and slept away from the water because his presence might have hindered other desert dwellers from approaching and drinking. Although the water level was too low now for any but Mouse to drink from the tank, when it was full, the tank, and another larger one twelve feet below, were used by all beings in the desert. None had exclusive privilege to the water; all had rights to life.

Mouse believed the tanks had been purposely created by the forces that shaped all things to provide a source of life in the Place of Birth. These forces first made the water basins, then formed the steep, rugged canyon to collect and channel rain water to fill them.

Mouse's tank was eleven feet deep. Its mouth yawned to three feet wide by seven feet long. The lower tank was twelve feet deep. Its opening was an oblong hole five feet wide by six feet long. When the fierce summer thunderstorms swept the desert, the rain poured down in sheets. The hot, crusty ground of the canyon, too dry to absorb the gushing moisture, funneled the water in a raging torrent to fill the basins, which were lower than the surrounding land. Full water tanks were a result of all things working in harmony; an act of benevolence by the forces of creation.

These same forces also were responsible when the tanks were emptied through constant use, evaporation, and infrequent or nonexistent thunderstorms. This too, Mouse accepted as part of the life process.

That there was water here in the Place of Birth, was a phenomenon to which the Southern Paiute had grown accustomed, but to which he was nevertheless still grateful and appreciative. One who lives close to the land learns the value of such things.

As Mouse awaited the coming of the light, he took a deep drink from his water gourd and thought of the tanks. He thanked all that shared the responsibility for the water; the rocks, the canyon, the earth, the clouds. He believed the Place of Birth was like no other and the water here was sacred. He had heard there was a place where there was so much water it rolled across the horizon the way the hills rolled across the skyline in the northern lands. Mouse thought these stories hard to believe even though he had been north and seen how much water was there. He had seen the vast blue lake in the north lands what held water so pure and cold it took his breath away.

Perhaps it was true about the water, he thought. It was certainly true that the differences in the land from one place to another were profound.

Where the southern desert lands were warm and inviting, in the north it was harder, colder, although undeniably a land of beauty. Mouse pictured the north where the white man's deeply rutted road traversed the state from east to west as a dusty, brittle strip of dry rabbit skin.

Mouse had been there once and had seen the lavish carpet of pale green sage and brittle yellow grass that covered much of the flowing landscape. In the north, swirls of color cross the horizon as waves on a static sea. The pungent currents and tides roll in increasing swells to crest in rugged, white-capped splendor on mountain peaks. Mouse had waded large, grassy, dark green islands in the north.

Islands that quilted areas of the countryside, revealing rips and tears where the white man had usurped the land and painstakingly carved niches to plant foreign seeds of alfalfa and grain. He had also seen the natural meandering lines of vigorous, lush grasses and waving river willows that revealed true water where the Mother of All had added ripples and eddies in the fabric of the dusty land-sea.

It truly was different; different and magnificent. But it was cold there, Mouse thought, much too cold for a Southern Paiute. These Nuwuvi needed the warmth of the Mojave Desert. They needed to feel the hot sun covering their dark shoulders with a yellow mantle that made the cleansing sweat pour from their bodies. Their eyes needed the rich red colors of life that tinted the rocks, the ground, and nearly all things in the southern lands. Their noses needed to smell the heat as it pressed lavish aromas from desert plants. And the Southern Paiutes needed to hear the scrunch, scrunch of footsteps as they walked the warm sandy carpets of home.

Mouse yawned deeply. It was good to be here and the day held promise. A promise that could only be realized by moving, by doing.

He sat up in the cave and reached into his gunnysack for his knife. After hanging the water carrier about his neck, he climbed out the narrow cave opening and stretched long and tall. The sun broke over the rocks and gentle beams flashed in his eyes. The cave was in such a place that the very early morning sun would light its doorway, but it would be in the shade the rest of the day. Mouse believed it was a place made from his mind.

He held his knife high and the rising sun streaked along its length. For the first time in many days, Mouse smiled not just in his heart, but with his heart, his eyes, his mouth, his being. This smile was an expression of the overwhelming joy of life. It was his nature; the nature of the People.

Mouse prayed to the new day and thanked the sun for coming back into his life and causing the darkness to flee. Though the sun was often hot and sometimes uncomfortable, it meant new life to the Southern Paiutes. It was a good thing .

The ledge in front of Mouse's cave was just big enough to hold the Southern Paiute and a tiny fire circle. He had made the circle in one corner of the ledge out of habit, but he had never lit a blaze there. There could be danger in a fire near where one slept as it could gather searching eyes the way it gathered moths in the velvet night.

Higher up the slope above his cave, wedged in a small crevice, Mouse had stacked piles of wood. He never intended to light a fire here, but Mouse was used to looking over his shoulder. Next to the fire circle was a pile of smooth stones. These stones had many uses, but today, they pointed only to the presence of man on the ledge.

Mouse slipped over the rim and carefully made his way down to the floor of the canyon. It was difficult only in that he did not want to leave an obvious trail to his stone home. The side of the gorge was strewn with rocks, large and small, and only the most experienced of eyes would be able to see Mouse's path.

He crossed the river of sand in the bottom of the canyon and walked a few steps up the other side. He pulled aside his breechclout and his strong yellow urine splashed wetly at the base of a creosote bush. In the desert, a full bladder and healthy spray meant water. Little water to drink meant little urine to release. It was good to have a strong spray in the early morning light.

Mouse was hungry and his thoughts turned to four traps he had set in the desert to catch food. Three were noose snares made with strings of rawhide he had strung invisibly in the middle of well-worn trails. On good days, the snares would trap and strangle unwary jackrabbits that raced through the desert oblivious to the strings.

The fourth trap was a small rock deadfall he had baited with a tiny piece of pinion pine nut from the meager handful in his gunnysack.

Although the pine nut was delicacy to the Southern Paiute, Mouse was willing to trade a small piece to supply himself with a breakfast of ground squirrel meat. It would be a fair trade.

He had set the deadfall close to a squirrel's underground home and thought that of all his traps it most probably would be successful. The succulent meat from the pine nut should draw the furry animal out of its burrow and Mouse would have breakfast.

His diet consisted of many things. The roots and leaves of many wild desert plants provided nourishment, as did all forms of desert mammals such as rabbits, squirrels and lizards. Even fat white grubs could be a tasty meal. Sparse flocks of desert bighorn sheep inhabited the scorched, brittle mountains around the Valley of Fire, and more than once Mouse and others of the People had trapped an animal in a box canyon and later feasted on its savory flesh.

Desert life was arduous and the rewards few, but it was a life relished by the Southern Paiutes. It was a life no white man seemed able to understand. The whites saw only the surface of desert life; the dryness, the heat, the meager diet. The important things to the Southern Paiute — the closeness of the People, the communal nature of life in the desert — seemed beyond their grasp. Yes, some of the things they brought were useful, like the knife. But mostly they were unwelcome intruders.

Mouse shook his head to dislodge these unwelcome thoughts and looked to the sky to fill his eyes first with the beauty of its blueness and then with visions of a meaty breakfast. As he made his way to the tank to fill his water gourd he thought if one of his traps had captured an animal, he would have to get there in a hurry or a hungry coyote, fox or turkey vultures would be eating his breakfast.

Mouse was one short step from the lip of the tank when a deadly buzzing shocked his attention from visions of roasted squirrel. His eyes flashed from the sky to the ground in front and to the left of his bare feet. There, tightly curled under a scraggly, broken piece of sage and poised to strike, was a sidewinder rattlesnake. Its tail was erect and the six bony rattles on the end were vibrating a venomous warning. Twin flaps of skin hooded the snake's eyes giving it an angry horned appearance.

The presence of the snake did not worry Mouse, especially since he was far enough away that the reptile rattled instead of striking. Rattlesnakes were familiar though unwelcome desert creatures.

An old tale told of how in the beginning of time, the rattlesnake, although one of the most beautiful of creatures, was jealous of all other beings because they walked on feet while he was forced to crawl on his belly. It whined and complained so long and so much that the creator, to appease the reptile, gave him twin lances that fired deadly poison. To protect others, however, the creator placed a rattle on the tail of the reptile that the snake should issue a warning before striking.

Had Mouse stepped on the snake, there would have been no warning, only the thud of the striking head and a burning sting, much hotter than the morning sun, as venom entered his body through long, sharp hollow fangs. As it was, Mouse believed himself safe. Confident in his knowledge of the ways of the desert, the Southern Paiute knew the rattler had only given notice not to proceed. With his eyes locked tightly on the deadly sidewinder, Mouse stepped quickly and smoothly to his right and the move put him out of the snake's reach — at least the snake on which his eyes were focused.

What Mouse had not seen was another dusty sidewinder lying at the base of the huge rock at the right side of the tank. His evasive step had put him squarely in the middle of that reptile's territory and it too issued an angry warning — a high buzzing that reminded Mouse of loud cicada. But there was no mistaking this furious sound for an insect. The snake quickly curled into a defensive position with its triangular head pulled back and cocked, ready to slam out and inject its toxin into the large intruder.

How curious it was, Mouse thought, that there should be two sidewinders so close together. Mouse knew these snakes had no permanent homes and wandered the desert sands like nomads. That there should be two, together in this place of water, was surely an omen.

Again, Mouse was not especially concerned about the snakes, believing there was nothing to worry about if he simply moved away. But then, as sometimes inexplicably happens, events occurred directly opposite of what was intended.

Mouse knew he need only move back in the direction he had come to get out of danger, but between his mind and his feet, the message became mixed. Instead of moving backward as he intended, his feet became flustered and Southern Paiute stepped forward. The stride put him on the gritty edge of the water tank. Without warning and with the same type of confusion that causes one to trip on a line etched in the sand, Mouse lost his balance and found himself falling headfirst into the watery depths of the tank. Time slowed until milliseconds seemed to last forever and a myriad of images flashed through his mind. Mouse's dark eyes narrowed to slits as he looked into the water-filled hole with a terror he had felt only one other time in his life.

Like all the children of the People in his band, Mouse had played in the waters of the Muddy, Virgin and Colorado rivers as long as he had been alive. In summer, the waters were torpid and shallow, providing a cooling playground for hot children weary of the seemingly endless heat. When Mouse was five, he was playing with the other children in the wide sluggish Muddy, when he stepped in a hole and plunged over his head in the dirty, silty river. The brown water filled his nose, mouth and even started trickling into his lungs before he was pulled gagging and retching from the hole.

The child eventually lost his fear of the water, but never the memory or the fear of drowning. Because of that, he never learned to swim more than a few strokes. That he might now dive to an agonizing death inside this smooth-sided water hole, was a horror to which he had no words to describe. Mouse knew the lethal nature of the tank from the number of sodden, lifeless animal bodies he had pulled from the water. Those which had crept too close when the water level was too low to allow a soothing drink.

Mouse threw his head back to shift momentum away from the tank and as he did, his feet slipped out from under his body and he crashed down on the rounded lip of the tank. When he hit the rock with the side of his body, the air whooshed from his lungs in a loud spray of air. In a breathless haze, Mouse felt himself slide toward the deep hole. Even in his stunned state, he could feel what was happening. He spun face down and the fingers of his left hand clawed at the hard stone on the edge of the tank. One fingernail tore off and Mouse's blood added a darker hue to the red of the rock. Inch by inch he was slipping into the hole.

Mouse became aware that in his right hand he still held his knife in its leather sheath. He wrenched it out, and with a desperate stab, he drove it deep into a crack in the rock on which he lay. The knife held and the Southern Paiute's backward slide into the tank stopped.

Mouse's mouth was agape and his eyes were tightly clenched as he fought to fill his lungs with air. The battle for breath was gut wrenching, made all the more difficult because of his position. From the hips down, his legs hung out over the water and his toes were just above the calm surface of the tank. Finally, with a straining gasp, air wheezed back into Mouse's lungs, and he was again able to breathe. The feeling was a spine-tingling sweetness that completely overshadowed the terror he had felt moments before. He had to make a conscious effort not to relax his taunt muscles to simply enjoy the feeling.

As he lay panting with his chest against the rock, dangling from his knife, he thanked the strong steel blade and the stone that provided the crack that held him. Mouse knew he had been lucky, but he also knew he was not yet out of danger and he had to get away from the lip of the tank. His palm was sweaty and slick, and his knuckles were white from the pressure of his hanging body. His face was pressed tightly against the rock and its warm earthiness filled his nostrils. Gently, with a soft, fluttery kicking motion he began to pull himself up over the lip of the hole; inch by inch he crept toward the flat land leading to the tank. He used his left hand to help pull himself up. He did not notice the throbbing ache where his fingernail had torn away.

Mouse was slowly making his way over the top of the warm rock when a familiar warning buzz shattered his concentration. Without moving another part of his tense body, the Southern Paiute slowly turned his head to look. What he saw soured the sweetness of his breath and turned his mouth to clay. The first sidewinder he had seen had slithered over and was curled eight inches from the hand that tightly wrapped the hilt of the knife. It was unbelievable that the snake had not fled after issuing its warning. Sidewinders were usually private creatures that would avoid man at all costs.

Mouse's face was close enough to the reptile to see how each individual scale overlapped its brother along the snake's body to create the smooth flaky skin. Mouse looked into hooded, unblinking eyes that were divided down the middle with a hairline pupil. The snake stared back at him as its split tongue flickered out to test the currents and flavors of the air.

In his imagination, Mouse could see the snake strike, its hollow fangs unfolding from the roof of its mouth to stab into Mouse's flesh and inject the toxin, and the terror the Southern Paiute felt was indescribable.

The bite of the Mojave Desert sidewinder is a terrible thing. It is one of the most toxic of rattlesnakes, and venom from the sidewinder primarily attacks the blood of its victim. Mouse had seen men of the People who had been bitten by the sidewinder survive, but not many. Those who had moved on to the other world had died an agonizing death.

Mouse knew he might survive a bite from the snake, especially if it struck a hand where the Southern Paiute could suck the poison from the wound, but the thought of a bite turned his stomach to an acid filled pit. Mouse wondered how long he could fight his natural reflexes to recoil from a strike and continue to hang from the knife. Or when the snake bit, would he release his grasp on the knife and fall into the tank?

His fear radiated from his body. He could feel it. He could smell it. The situation seemed hopeless, but Mouse was a Southern Paiute; a member of the People fighting for lands that had been overrun and claimed by an invading hoard. He was inured to hopeless situations. By his reasoning, his only defense was to outlast the snake, so as best he could, he settled himself to wait. And as he waited, Mouse began to sing to the angry rattler in a low whispery voice he knew the snake would understand.

He sang a song of life and of the brotherhood of desert dwellers, and of all the reasons the angry sidewinder should not strike. In his song, he told the snake the story of how he had come to be in the Place of Birth on this hot summer day. He told of the knife and how it was not unlike the twin lances the sidewinder carried in its own mouth. And as the moments passed and the song progressed, the snake calmed. The rattling tail gentled and then stopped altogether.

In a moment, Mouse, too, stopped singing and the quiet in the clearing was deafening. The rock under the Southern Paiute was dark with his sweat and his tight muscles were trembling from the strain of supporting his body.

The snake remained motionless and quiet for another instant and then began slowly slithering away in the unique looping fashion of the sidewinder. The smooth scales of the snakes belly were rougher than the smooth sand in the clearing and they grated with a dry, harsh rasp as the rattler left. A grateful Mouse immediately began kicking again, inching his way up the sloped rock. He pulled himself past the knife in the crack and his toes gained a purchase. He pulled and pushed and wriggled and finally tugged himself over the top. Lying prone in the hot sand, he silently thanked all he could think of for his life. How sweet the moment to have escaped the tank. The sun already seemed scalding, but Mouse believed nothing had ever felt better. He was alive and it was good. But where there is sweet, there is also sour.

As the Southern Paiute rolled over to climb to his feet, he felt a light ticklish thud and a sharp burn in the muscle of his back behind his right arm. He immediately threw his body away from the pain and scrambled to his feet. Looking down, Mouse could see the second sidewinder where it lay coiled on the sand. Like the white man, it had struck without a warning; its rattle curiously silent. Mouse had rolled on top of the snake and it had bit him, sinking sharp hollow fangs into his flesh and injecting its deadly fluid into his body. The bite had lighted a fire in his back.

For only an instant, Mouse looked down at the snake and wondered at the quirks of destiny. That fate should be so enigmatic as to have caused the unlikely events of the morning was surely beyond the comprehension of a simple Southern Paiute. But Mouse had no time to wonder for long. He shook his head and retrieved his knife from the crack in the rock.

He knew he had no time to waste if he were to live, for the burn in his back was spreading. He walked quickly back up the canyon toward his cave unmindful of the deep footprints his feet left in the soft sand.

Chapter Seven

Mouse prepared a fire in the circle of stones on the ledge outside his small cave. His hands quivered as he placed tiny bone-dry mesquite twigs in a small pile next to the remnants of a bird's nest he had plucked from a tall tree. Nearby were larger branches of mesquite and some green boughs of sage and creosote. The sage and creosote were sacred and medicinal. The smoke they released as they burned would help in the battle for life. It was not a good thing to have a fire so close, but all things must rely on circumstances.

The Southern Paiute bent over his fire circle and

struck a small piece of flint with the back edge of his knife. The strike produced a hot spark that jumped from a ridge on the shiny black stone to the bird's nest. It flared brightly but failed to hold. Three more strikes produced three more sparks, but again, none held long enough to ignite the nest. Mouse was trembling and the urgency of his actions and the poison in his system made him clumsy.

It had been only twenty minutes since the snake struck, but already the burn from the bite behind his arm had spread until he felt the pain from his waist to the thick muscle that led from his shoulder to his neck. His right arm was hugely swollen, and nausea rose in waves from his stomach. Sidewinder venom is very powerful, but it was a good sign that he was still moving. It was also proof of the Southern Paiute's will to live. Mouse wished he could take the heat from his body and place it in the bird's nest where it would quickly light the fire.

He concentrated on the second of two more sparks which landed and held bright yellow in the fuzzy nest. With both hands he gently cupped the bird's nest around the spark and, like the creator pushing breath into a fresh life, blew softly into its middle. A thin tendril of gray smoke rose from the nest and Mouse placed the mass in the circle of stones and covered it with the twigs of Mesquite. Another gentle blow and a tiny yellow flame sprang up in the midst of the smoke and began eating the wood.

Mouse collapsed on his left side and watery vomit trickled from his mouth and puddled in the sand. Slowly it soaked into the ground and left a dark patch. He lay beside the small fire and stared with large, black pupils into the ever increasing flames. His entire face was pale, but the area around his mouth appeared lighter than the rest of his skin and it tingled. The bite on his back had become massive, the muscle swollen to an immense mound that was excruciatingly painful. The outside air lay against the throbbing tenderness like salt in a raw wound. With his left hand he pressed the sides of the area where he had been bitten by the sidewinder. A bloody fluid oozed out and the pain made him retch again.

As he had walked from the clearing in front of the water tanks, Mouse had used his sharp knife to carefully cut a shallow slice into the muscle across the twin holes where the snake's fangs had entered. His probing hand had served as his eyes since the bite was too far back for him to see. Mouse had cautiously made the cut, then pressed on the sides of the area to squeeze out as much venom as he could. He hoped his flowing blood would wash the poison from the wound. Even as he had walked from the tanks the area on his back was painful to the touch.

Not all bites from Mohave Desert sidewinders are fatal. In some cases such as when the snake strikes out as protection, no venom is released into the wound. Mouse knew, however, that there was no doubt this bite was serious and toxin had been injected. The burning pain, the swelling and the tingling around his mouth told him he had been poisoned. The snake's venom had immediately began attacking Mouse's blood and, to a lesser degree, his nervous system. Mouse was very sick. He could only hope the poison was not enough to kill him.

It was just mid morning as the fire consumed the fragrant mesquite and sage. Smoke from the fire rose in a heavy, swirling line that Mouse inhaled deeply into his lungs. The smoke began to mark a dark line up the wall of the canyon.which would be there for all time. Mouse selected three smooth stones from the pile by the fire circle and placed them in the blaze to get hot. These stones were different from the other rocks in the Place of Birth. They had the look and feel of the rocks found in the bottom of the Muddy River. They were rounded, very smooth, and, like Mouse, had tight, tight pores.

Mouse believed the rocks were from the other time when the Place of Birth was covered by water. The Southern Paiutes knew of this water because of legends passed down since the beginning of time and because of the tiny water-creature shells found on the sides of mountains. The shells proved the truth of the legends — had any proof been needed.

As soon as Mouse climbed to his ledge, he had prepared a small leather bag in which he had placed some water and leaves of sage, creosote and willow. The sage and creosote, as well as some shadescale, he had picked on his way up the canyon after being bitten. The willow he had inside his gunnysack.

In few moments the rocks in the fire were hot and Mouse propped himself up. Using two dried sticks, he transferred a hot rock to the small sack. It hissed and began heating the water in the bag. In a moment, he replaced the stone with another from the fire, and that one with another. Thus, the tea in the bag was brewed. Mouse cupped the bag to his mouth and took a long sip. The sharp bitter tang of the tea flared in his stomach and he vomited it to the ground. He immediately took another sip and this one stayed down. He knew he must keep this acrid fluid in his stomach if it was going to help him live.

Mouse pulled from his gunnysack the white man's shirt given to him by the Mormons. He carefully folded it around the sodden leaves from his leather bag of tea. He added some fresh leaves from the branches he had picked of sage, creosote and shadescale and then folded the cloth carefully around the leaves. This wet packet would be a poultice to sooth his wound, fight infection and help draw the snake venom from his body.

The Southern Paiute lay on the sand and stared into his small fire. He reached up under his right arm and pressed the damp package on his wound. Pain made him moan and vomit trickled from his mouth. He could smell the bitter dampness of the desert where his vomit created a dark spot. Mouse could feel his heart fluttering in his chest. He heard the sound of his blood streaming through his veins. He tried to put the pain from mind, but succeeded only in bringing it to the forefront of his consciousness. Like a million stinging pricks from a spiny cactus, the tingling around his mouth began to spread. The feeling was in his tongue now; it moved down his throat, across his chest and into his hands. It crept into his nose, and around his eyes and ears.

As the tingling spread, a murky darkness began to overwhelm the Southern Paiute. Lying helpless and weak in the sand, pain pounding in the depths of his being and strings of vomit dripping from his mouth, Mouse feebly watched a filmy curtain obscure the flame of his fire. Slowly, slowly and ever so painfully, shadows engulfed the light. At first Mouse fought the shadows and the profound sense of loss, of doom, raging in his chest.

He wanted desperately to live and the thought of dying here, alone in the Place of Birth, was like a heavy stone that lay next to his heart. He could taste a metallic fear and it churned his stomach. Mouse watched the darkness slowly closing in and he believed death was coming to claim his soul. He prepared himself and tried to sing, but no sound came from his mouth and his lips did not move.

To give in filled him with a sense of despair, but in the darkness the pain was not so bad, the tingling not so demanding, and Mouse finally gave up and wrapped himself in its soothing softness. In a few moments, the pain raging under the poultice eased a bit. The wound had accepted the presence of the medicine; much better than his stomach had accepted the tea. He grunted as he lifted his head and took another sip of the strong mixture.

In the velvety blackness, Mouse's hurt faded until it was only a nagging pull at his back. Then it was gone. One moment it was there, and then next it was not. Awareness came like a pleasing sound at the edge of his consciousness and he cocked his head to listen. The loss of pain was as a calming, gentle voice of a mother to her baby; the tinkling, carefree laughs of distant children lost in the sheer delight of life; the satisfied moans of a Southern Paiute couple sharing the joy of life. This must be death, Mouse thought. Perhaps I have finished my time in the place that was and have started the journey to the place that will be. He tried to look around but could see, sense, only the darkness.

But Mouse was aware of himself. He heard and felt his heart beat strongly and loudly. It beat with the steady cadence of the circle dance drum and the blood whooshed in his veins. He felt free, released from the earthly ties of pain. Mouse's eyes were open but the blackness and the peace were total. It was good here.

Far away in the darkness, Mouse could see a tiny spot of light; a star in the blackness slowing moving toward him with a bright intensity. The spot of light began skipping and cavorting in time to the drumbeat in Mouse's chest and the Southern Paiute found he had to dance to keep the light in view. He danced left, right, up, down, front, back. The light moved and Mouse moved with it. As the light grew, he could see it was not just a spot, but a being; a being with stick arms, stick legs, a headdress of many flashing rays and in one hand, a blazing knife. Light spewed from the tip of the knife as from the sun, and Mouse squinted as the light flashed in his eyes. In his heart, the heart that beat like a drum, he knew that this was the creator.

Mouse danced and spun and watched the being and mimicked his every step, every spin, every move. At first, he tried to ask where was this place, but there were no words with which to question, so he danced and the stick being of light became his shadow and danced with him. Mouse felt good and laughed. It was exhilerating to dance with a friend; dance and feel the beat of life in his feet, in his head, in his soul.

As they moved to the rhythm of Mouse's heart, the flashing knife held by the creator began to make designs in the darkness. The designs were those etched upon the rocks in the Place of Birth — a rotating spiral that sparkled and turned and fed upon itself; waves across the land that rippled in a sinewy, never-ending flowing; the portentous crossroads at which the People were faced with the choices that designed their destinies; a myriad of animal shapes, one of which was repeated over and over. It was the horse. It must be Sheriff John Currie's horse, Mouse thought.

The drawings had meaning and Mouse understood — finally. The designs were not merely pages from the book of life, they were life. They did not just say where to go, but that there were many ways to get there. The continuity of existence; the happenstance of life; all things were in these shapes and drawings.

Mouse looked down at himself and found he too was a stick being. His searching hands found a sparkling headdress atop his head and his eyes found a knife flashing in his hand. Designs began to spout in a glimmering eruption from the tip of his knife. He could see there was a pattern and he was part of the pattern. He felt the power of the knife in his hand and knew he could make his own designs within the framework of the already existing pattern of life.

All things began to flare from Mouse's knife. The story of Mouse the Southern Paiute was written across the blackness in a twinkling torrent of fire. How powerful it felt to draw the pictures that had been the life, that was the life, and that would be the life. With five strokes, Mouse drew the picture of the horse. And as the animal streamed from the tip of his knife, Mouse sprang upon its back and rode the black wind among the gleaming patterns of life.

The power of the horse pulsed through Mouse's thighs and into his blood. As the horse raced with the wind, Mouse felt its power course through his body giving him its vitality of life. He could feel the heart of the animal, and it began beating in time to his own. They were as one, and the strength of the horse became the strength of Mouse, the Southern Paiute.

Mouse decided he would stay here forever and light the way for others by riding the horse and drawing destiny with his blazing knife. He would dance to the beat of his heart and others would come and understand. The designs he drew with his streaking knife mingled with those of the other being and marked the fate of the world. It was good.

But it was not to be. The horse began to dim. Its power faded and Mouse felt the strong, sleek muscles of the animal melt and disappear and he found himself dancing again. He began to tire for it seemed he had been dancing for a long time. How long he did not know, but it was very long time and he was weak. The other figure in the blackness danced and spun and the pictures that flashed from its brilliant knife outshone those drawn by Mouse. This being did not grow tired. It was more powerful and it was drawing the destiny by which Mouse would live. There were shapes, beings, images that Mouse knew would affect his life. But it was too much to understand; too much, too fast and he was lost.

As the blaze of understanding left Mouse's mind, he watched a creeping scorpion crawl from the other's knife. The insect's front claws were held wide apart and its poison-tipped tail was curled over its back. The scorpion's tiny black eyes flashed at Mouse and he knew there was a message there, but he could not understand. Was there a message of life held in the gaping claws? Or something else?

Mouse's knife began to fade and the pictures it had drawn became fuzzy and dim. Mouse could no longer read them and he was unsure of what designs he should be making. Those he had first drawn were still bright but after the scorpion he could no longer make new ones. The power he had felt became a memory, and Mouse realized he was not ready for this place. His fate was sealed in the pictures drawn by the other.

The stick being began to dance away. It grew smaller and smaller until again it was only a bright spot in the distance. Then it winked out and Mouse was alone in the darkness in the middle of a flowing pattern. What had been was clear. But what was, or what would be, Mouse was not certain. He knew only that he had a destiny — a destiny irrevocably etched in the black stone of this place.

After a time in the darkness, light slowly began to intrude into Mouse's consciousness. First he was aware only of the blackness, then the black was gray, then it was light, and Mouse realized he was reborn. He was slipping from the comfort of the place of darkness into the life that had been. The life that was the Place of Birth.

And with the light came pain. Not the pain that lived in his memory, but a steady throbbing that was not so bad. Mouse opened his eyes and looked out into the familiar fiery brilliance of a new day. It was morning, he was alive, and he was home in his cave on the ledge. And despite the dull incessant throbbing in his body, it was good.

Chapter Eight

The powdery sand of his small cave felt downy under Mouse's body. It conformed to his shape and cradled him in its soft redness. A dazzling morning sun peeked over the distant boulders and flashed brightly in the entrance. Today, the warm yellow lances felt like gentle, massaging fingers. They bathed his face with the welcome feeling of life.

Mouse had awakened with instant awareness; no questions, no confusion. He knew exactly where he was and what had happened. He did not know how long he had been on the ledge, but it did not matter. He was alive and his life would go on. That he had survived the virulent bite of a Mojave Desert sidewinder gave him immense pride.

Mouse believed it was evidence of his power, but it was no great tribute to him; merely a fact that was. All desert dwellers fight tenaciously for life, and he had not forgotten he could just have easily have died. Existence in the scalding Mojave was arduous and a never-ending chore, albeit a welcome one. This was to be another day, just as the day before and the day before that. But Mouse grunted with satisfaction; it was a good feeling to be alive and to have beaten one of the most powerful creatures in his world.

A stench filled the cave and Mouse knew it was his body and his excretions. The rankness of the fetid air told the Southern Paiute he had been laying here for more than a few days. It smelled much like the St. Thomas jail and the odor made Mouse smile. How pleasurable it was to fill his nose with this foulness and feel the pain in his body.

Slowly, gingerly Mouse tested his body. He carefully worked his right shoulder in delicate, imperceptible circles to feel the pain. It hurt, but not the sharp, intense agony like white-hot lances firing through his body. It was only the achy dull pain of a healing wound. He clenched his fists and then his toes. He stretched the muscles of his legs and moved his feet just enough to tell him they would move when commanded. With his left hand he probed the bite on his back and felt the crust of ooze and pus that coated the area. Although some of the swelling was gone, Mouse could feel the wound was still sore and puffy with a deep depression in the middle.

Mouse clenched his teeth and pressed on the sides of the pit in his muscle. He felt the crusty scab break and the flow of fluid from the wound — some blood, some pus. The action covered his body with a heavy film of sweat and made him weak. After a moment nothing more oozed from the wound and Mouse stopped pressing. He rested and in a while the sore dried over.

The Southern Paiute knew he had been only a breath from dying and was still in danger. Having survived the first part of the ordeal was a tribute to what he had been when the snake struck. He would need to eat, drink and rebuild himself if he was to continue to live.

Resting on his left side, Mouse looked out at the ledge and could see his fire was out. The leather bag in which he had made his tea and the once-white shirt that had held his poultice were lying on the ledge outside the fire pit. The shirt was heavily spotted and appeared stiff with a fetid crust. He had used the poultice several times to draw the poison from his body and he marveled at his own will to live.

He could not remember crawling from the fire circle into the cave. He felt thirsty and was looking around his dusty bed for the water gourd when a dark shape slammed into the ground outside causing Mouse's already dry mouth to pucker and his heart to beat wildly.

Confused for only an instant, however, he recognized the intruder was merely a very large turkey vulture that had landed upon the ledge. One bare talon was buried deep in the lifeless side of a brown, gray and white mottled jackrabbit — surprising since the vulture's feet are not well developed for grasping prey. That this bird should land on Mouse's ledge with a dead animal clenched in a foot was astounding.

In seconds, another vulture joined the first and they began fighting over the hare's carcass. The bright redness of their bald heads flashed at one another and their bulging beady eyes were like fire. The second bird used both feet to claw out at the first, which hopped backward, dragging the dead hare toward the mouth of Mouse's cave. The scratch from their talons was raspy on the rock of the ledge and Mouse could hear their beaks clack as they struck at one another. Their feathers rustled loudly as they fought for the prize.

Despite the stink in his own lair, Mouse could smell the big birds as they flapped three-foot wings at one another in the early morning. In hot weather, turkey vultures direct their excrement to spray against their legs to cool themselves. Between grooming periods, the spray and the splash from the fluid can accumulate in the under-feathers of the birds. The stench can be very strong — even to one who had been lying in his own filth for many days.

As the battle for the dead hare continued, the first bird retreated until the fight raged just outside the cave's entrance. Mouse's mind was sluggish, but he knew the value of the dead black-tailed jackrabbit. As fast as his arm could move, the Southern Paiute reached out and with a croaking yell, grabbed the long hind legs of the hare. He pulled as hard as he could.

His back muscle, damaged by the sidewinder bite, screamed in protest and Mouse nearly retched from the burning pain, but he held onto the furry carcass which he pulled from the claw of the flapping vulture. The angry bird shrieked in surprise then leaped from the ledge with a flash of heavy dark wings. The second bird immediately joined the first and Mouse was again alone.

The body of the jackrabbit was supple and Mouse knew it had not been dead long. He could see where strong jaws, perhaps of a coyote, had clamped on the neck of the animal drawing a spot of bright, shiny blood on the fur. When Mouse touched it with his finger, it smeared onto his skin. It was strange that the kill was so fresh, Mouse thought, since vultures prefer their meals to be ripened in the hot desert sun for at least a day or two. Maybe there were other forces at work and the animals were working together to keep him alive. The jackrabbit offered its body; the coyote killed it, and the vultures delivered it to the Nuwuvi man who was too weak to hunt. All signs told Mouse this was the true course of events.

His eyes squinted in concentration as he worked out the scenario. It made sense. Mouse's life was valuable in the scheme of the desert. Had he not survived the snakebite? Had he not danced with the creator and created a pattern of life for himself and for others? Yes, Mouse thought, this is exactly what happened and it would be his story of life. It was good feeling to feel the camaraderie of others and know he was not alone. He thanked the hare, the coyote, and the vultures. He thanked the creator and thought about the strangeness of life as he prepared to eat.

Although Mouse's knife was stuck in the dirt to one side of the cave's entrance, he did not use it. With practiced hands he twisted and worked the skin at the base of hare's four legs until it separated. Then he gently tore the fur at the anus of the animal, gradually enlarging the hole until he could pull and slip the whole skin off the body and over the head of the jackrabbit. Eventually he was left with a naked carcass of dark red meat on which there were four furry socks.

The sight and bloody smell of the meat made the saliva run in Mouse's mouth and spill over his chin. With strong white teeth he began stripping the flesh from the body. Nothing had ever tasted so good. The meat was stringy, strong and delicious.He fought the temptation to swallow the heavily muscled meat in whole chunks that he ripped from the hare. He knew if he were to keep the food in his stomach, he would have to chew thoroughly and swallow small portions. He desperately needed the nourishment and he did not want to vomit again.

After consuming only a small portion of the carcass, Mouse could eat no more and he relaxed. The rest of the meat he placed on his gunnysack sitting at the head of his soft bed inside the cave. The hare would give him two, maybe three more meals. He could feel the meat heavy in his stomach and it was a good feeling; a feeling of life.

He found his water gourd partially buried in the sand behind him with a cupful sloshing in the bottom. Mouse sipped slowly at the stale fluid until it was nearly gone saving a mouthful for later. With food and water, Mouse would grow strong and live.

He dozed as he lay contented in his powdery bed and the images of the other place cavorted behind his closed eyes. He remembered being in that place and dancing to the beat of his heart. He remembered the horse, the feeling of power and wonder as the designs spewed from his flaming knife when he rode across the face of the black wind. In his mind he watched the patterns shimmer in splendor across the horizon and he rode the horse and felt its strength. That he had been marking the future filled him with a reverence for the things that were to come, although he was unsure what that meant.

But in the back of his mind, Mouse also remembered the burn in his body from the strike of the dusty Mojave Desert sidewinder. He remembered his feelings of impotence and confusion when the snake had sunk sharp, venomous fangs into his back. He recalled the flight up the canyon, the fear of death and the metallic taste of that fear in his mouth. Being alive, here in the Place of Birth, was a good thing, but Mouse realized that life on this plane was fleeting and tenuous, and he longed for the power of the other place; the power of the horse.

Memories, thoughts and shimmering patterns swirled in a mass inside Mouse's head. The mass was like the unformed gray, clay ooze on the bottom of the Muddy River. He turned the ooze over and over in his mind, running his mental fingers through its bulk; wondering, questioning, thinking.

He opened his eyes and looked across the red sand outside his cave. Heavy furrows lined his forehead. Through the foul odors of the cave, Mouse could smell the clean richness of the Place of Birth.

He took his knife from the dirt and held it out in the sun. The light sparkled off the sharp blade and flashed patterns in his eyes and on the walls inside his small cave. He moved the knife in a sinuous dance and the glittering light created wondrous designs not unlike those of the other place. In the designs Mouse could see the horse; the horse that would take him into the future on its broad back.

As he imagined this thing, Mouse mentally explored his body from his feet to his head, then back again. He flexed his toes, his fingers and he clenched his buttocks. He tightened his back and felt the pain of the snakebite. This is the body and the knife of the other place Mouse thought, and I will get the horse with all these things and I will draw my own future.

The realization of the power he held was a dawning like the brilliance of the morning sun, and as he lay in the red dust of his small cave, Mouse began to replay an earlier plan by which he would take the horse, and in the taking, outsmart the whites who had invaded his land and claimed it for their own. With his mental hands and fingers he began to mold and craft the ooze of his thoughts into a shape of the way things would be.

Mouse could do these things, he thought, because he was Nuwuvi. He had survived the bite of a Mojave Desert sidewinder and he was powerful. Mouse believed because he held his fate, and the fate of others, in his own hands he would fashion a path through the coming years and it would be written in the rocks of this place — the Place of Birth — and it would be good.

But Mouse had forgotten the white man. He had forgotten that their lives intertwined with the lives of the People in a tangle that made little sense to the Nuwuvi. He had forgotten that the whites sometimes moved at odds with the way things had been written. And he had forgotten that, like the Mojave Desert sidewinder, they could strike.

Chapter Nine

From the bottom of the sandy canyon, Mouse scrutinized the ledge on which his cave was located and the area on the side of the canyon that led to the ledge. He looked for footprints he had not hidden, a disturbed rock; a broken stem of dry yellow grass; any sign that might suggest recent human presence. Time after time he had gone up and down the canyon slope disguising and covering the marks and tracks he had made while living moment to moment on this ledge. Mouse had been methodical and meticulous; brushing here, replacing this stone, pulling out and taking unsettled grass.

He had captured two small lizards early that morning and these he herded with a long stick in a scampering trek over the sand he had first patiently smoothed. The unmistakable trails made by the tiny reptiles would hide a multitude of other sign.

It took much work to hide his presence, but this place was too convenient and comfortable a home to allow an intruder to learn of its location. It was too close to the tank. A curious mind might wonder why someone would repeatedly camp on the barren ledge. The curious mind would wonder and then begin a search that would reveal the tank.

After a careful inspection, Mouse was convinced he had done well, although toward the rear of the ledge he could see faint marks where he had scrubbed with a rough, fist-size rock of granite to remove the black line that pointed from his fire circle up the steep wall of the canyon. He had scoured away the dark smoke mark from the rock and then took sand from the canyon floor and rubbed it into the scratches that had been left behind. But a faint shadow remained where he had worked. Mouse decided that only the most experienced of eyes, looking up from the bottom of the canyon at exactly the right angle, with the sun at a precise point in the sky, would detect there had been a fire on the ledge. And even then, most would think the fire sign a remnant of the ancient hunters in this place.

Mouse brushed the dirt from his hands and wiped the sweat that had trickled from under his headband. Finally satisfied with the appearance of the site, he started up the canyon away from his tank. His firm, precise steps scrunched in the sand and he relished the sound. Temperatures were on the downside of the day's high of 111 degrees, but it was still very hot. As much as possible, he walked on rocks that lay in shade along the sides of the fiery canyon. He checked the sun hanging low in the western sky. He believed it would take him a little more than three hours to walk to St. Thomas, which would put him in town at dusk.

Mouse had tied the scabbard of his knife to a loop made of the laces from the shoes the Mormons had given him. He slung the loop around his neck and under his left shoulder then tucked it into the side of his breechclout so it didn't flop against his side. This way his hands were free and the knife was ready at hand. The knife sheath no longer looked new and had many small scratches from the sand. The knife had become as much a part of Mouse as an arm a leg, or a tooth.

Hanging from another cord below the knife was Mouse's water gourd. He once would have arrogantly walked the blistering desert trail to St. Thomas with no water, but he had become aware of his limitations. The rattlesnake seemed to have injected logic and some common sense along with its venom. Mouse was older, more cautious after his fight for life.

By his reckoning, it had been two weeks since his encounter with the sidewinder. He felt better each day, although the wound behind his right arm had not completely healed and it often wept foul pus that Mouse absentmindedly wiped away with his left hand. The Southern Paiute had several times pressed the sides of the snakebite to clean out the wound, but it remained dry for only a short time. Four days ago, in his small fire, he had heated the blade of his knife to a glowing white. He stuck the shimmering blade in the hole to cauterize the wound, but it did not work and the next morning it was again weeping. He believed the sore would eventually close, and until then, he would ignore the irritating ache that had become his constant companion. The large dent in his back where the venom had destroyed part of his muscle he would have for the rest of his life. The deep scar told a harrowing story of Mouse's fight for existence. He would, with pride, forever turn his back to friend and foe alike.

Mouse felt strong and confident as he started toward St. Thomas thinking often about the horse and Sheriff John Currie with his booming pistol. He hoped Currie had not taken the animal and returned to Searchlight, or Las Vegas, or some other white man town.

Perhaps the sheriff traveled by train to Las Vegas, Mouse thought. Mouse had been in Las Vegas and had seen the problems there. Dusty miners and railroad workers clashing in dirt-floored saloons after hot words were ignited to flashing flames from splashes of whiskey. If Currie had gone to Las Vegas, maybe he left the big bay horse to rest in the shade under the cottonwood trees in St. Thomas.

It didn't matter, Mouse reasoned, for if Currie had left town with the horse, he would be back. Then Mouse would steal into town with the feet of a ghost, take the horse, and steal out. The missing animal would be the only sign of his presence. One way or another, sooner or later, Mouse would get the horse.

He was panting slightly and was covered with a fine film of sweat by the time he reached the clearing in the mouth of the canyon. The snake had sapped more of his strength than he wanted to admit. It would be a long march to the Muddy River. Mouse swept the last of his footprints from the canyon entrance, checked his back-trail one more time and started out across the desert.

As Mouse walked he felt and tasted a hint of change floating on the desert breeze. He sipped the sweetness of the air and smelled the gentle currents that held a promise of something new. Although the sun was a fireball in the sky and still poured relentless heat down upon the Mojave Desert, far in the west a round ball of a cloud bobbed high above the mountains and Mouse read that sign as an an omen knowing the tempo of the desert was about to change.

Four grueling hours later, the sun turned the sky crimson as it dipped below the blazing hills west of St. Thomas. Long black caricatures, stretching across the ground from the bottoms of reality, had begun to join and melt into one vast smear of darkness. An exhausted Mouse plopped in the sand on the outskirts of town.

Late July evenings meant easier temperatures, a time for taking deep breaths of cooling air and Mouse was ready. He was spent. The walk from the Place of Birth had sucked the strength from his body the way he sucked water from his gourd. Mouse would rest and wait for the night to become whole.

The few St. Thomas citizens who lived in town proper, often gathered after sundown to discuss the long hot days; but not today. Today, Mouse was lucky. It was the middle of the week and sundown today in this farming community of Mormons meant supper, evening prayers and welcome beds after a long, arduous day in the Mojave Desert heat.

There were perhaps forty-five residents who lived in St. Thomas. Most were of hardy stock, proud of their homes and farms on the banks of the Muddy River; the homes and farms they had scratched into the fertile ground of the river bottoms once occupied by the Southern Paiutes. More than one farmer made grateful use of an irrigation ditch the Nuwuvi had painstakingly carved into the desert soil with sticks and flat pieces of river drift wood two hundred years before the Mormons ever laid eyes on the Muddy River.

The Mormons had first come to Southern Nevada in the 1850s. Dispatched by the Mormon hierarchy to build a mission to ensure safe passage between California and Utah, a line of tiny settlements stretched from Salt Lake City all the way to the Las Vegas Valley and beyond. In 1855, in the lush grasses of the verdant natural meadows named Las Vegas, the Mormons built a fort. It was later abandoned to bake and crumble in the harsh desert air.

Some years later, in 1865, a group of Mormons led by Brother Thomas Smith moved down from Utah to grow cotton in the warm southern climate to help in the war effort of the day. The Mormons had no quarrel with the Nuwuvi, but seeing the land around the Muddy River vacant, they believed it without ownership. So they took it for their own, built a town and named it St. Thomas after their stalwart leader. The town thrived, with houses, barns and buildings springing up, and the Mormons took pride in their accomplishments. In churches built to last, they thanked their God for the land and the crops.

Politics would later force the Mormons to abandon their Southern Nevada communities, and many farms were expropriated, in just the manner that the Mormons had usurped the land from the Southern Paiutes. They later returned, however, and many righteously reclaimed the land they considered their own. They took back much of the land, the town and many of the buildings, including the St. Thomas jail.

One hundred yards from that jail Mouse sat motionless, resting near the muted edge of a growing shadow. He had only a splash of water left in his gourd. It had been a long walk from the Valley of Fire and he was grateful for the time to rest.

His dark skin blended smoothly with the coming night and he was nearly invisible to any who might have looked, but no one looked. The stench of the jail wafted thickly over the warm ground and Mouse wondered if those who lived in this place ever got tired of the foreign stench of confinement. Perhaps living closed up in their houses made the aroma not as foul to the Mormons as it was to him.

As the night deepened, a patient Mouse watched lights blink out in the homes he could see. One by one, lanterns or candles would sweep from one window to the next in the small houses, waver briefly, then blink into quiet darkness.

Mouse watched the lights disappear in the homes of the Prisbeys, the Gibsons, Murphys, Nays and finally the Bunkers.

The Bunkers lived in a house behind their general store in the middle of town; the store from which Mouse had stolen his life-saving knife. The business had started out in a one-room wooden summer kitchen that had housed the family while a permanent brick and stone home was constructed. After the walls were up on the main house, Bunker had turned the summer kitchen into the general store. It was kept stocked with goods that arrived from Salt Lake City, San Francisco and Los Angeles. The goods came by train, wagon and riverboats steaming up the Colorado River.

To turn the summer kitchen into a store, Bunker had constructed a wide, tall panel across the front of the building. The false front gave the impression that the store was a large emporium, much bigger than it actually was. A store room and office were eventually added to the back of the building, making it in truth, the biggest building in St. Thomas. The part that faced the Southern Paiutes who came to purchase goods, however, remained false.

Like all things in the Mojave, the store and the goods inside were dusty. When hot desert winds blasted across the landscape in rolling waves, it carried sand unfettered into the minute cracks and crevices of the wooden building. The dust covered merchandise in the store with a dry, powdery icing. Despite the dirt and the heavy odor of dust, however, the things inside the store smelled new, unused and compelling. The hoes and shovels leaning in one corner were sharp, eager for willing hands. The inner surfaces of the bolts of cloth, the surfaces that the dust could not reach, were crisp and smooth, begging for transformation from cloth to clothes.

The store was a place like no other and the Nuwuvi loved to smell the newness of the goods. The younger Southern Paiutes who had grown up with the presence of the store, accepted it for what it was. But the elders could not understand why all these things were kept in one wooden building when there was such a great need for them outside the building. Why keep three axes stacked in a corner when wood was always needed to feed the fires of the People? It made little sense. These whites were a confusing people.

Bunker would not allow the Southern Paiutes into his store unless they first showed the money with which they would pay for goods. Even then, the store owner made them describe exactly what they wanted before entering the store. He allowed them only to touch the things they were going to purchase, believing the desert dust on Southern Paiute hands dirtier than the desert dirt on white hands.

There was little cash in St. Thomas, and much of the purchasing of goods by Mormons in the community was done by bartering, giving one thing for another; a dozen eggs for a comb to pull the morning snarls from a woman's hair, a ton of hay for the tools with which to harvest it. Bunker would barter with the Southern Paiutes, especially for the fine baskets woven by the Nuwuvi women, but mostly he told them they had to have money to purchase goods in his store.

Much of the money in St. Thomas came from settlers passing through the small town on their way south to California. Of all the families in town, the Bunkers had more cash than any other due to the nature of their life. Bunker was well thought of in St. Thomas. The Mormons are respectful of men who have money.

Attached to the rear of the Bunker home, over the back door, was a small wooden lean-to. Like the jail, it had one tiny window to let in light during the day. The outside door to the lean-to opened to the east, as a proper door should. The brick of the main house had been painted a pale yellow, but the wood on the small addition remained stark; weathered, dry and splintery. In several spots on the outside wall, cracks between boards had been chinked with mud to keep the outside out and the inside in. A piece of cloth had been hung in front of the small window in the lean-to and Mouse could see a flickering splash of light through its texture.

Quiet as his namesake, Mouse crept under the window and stood pressed against the side of the building listening. He had been there only a moment when the light went out. He tiptoed to the door and scratched lightly on its weathered surface. There was no response, so he scratched harder. He heard a shuffle inside the lean-to and a low question.

"It is Mouse," he whispered in the voice of the People. "I must talk to you. Let me in."

In a moment the door slowly creaked open just enough for Mouse to slip inside. It closed behind him and for the first time in weeks, Mouse was no longer alone.

Chapter Ten

The darkness inside the lean-to was dense. Mouse could see only shadows of the things in the room and the black silhouette of the person inside. The cloth over the window blocked most of the thin moonlight outside. There was a rustle, a raspy scratching sound and light flared as the heavy odor of sulfur filled the small space.

Morning Blossom, a 16-year-old Southern Paiute girl who lived in the lean-to, lit a stubby candle standing erect in a small tin can that once held sweet fruit. She blew out the match and faced Mouse, waiting for him to speak. The yellow light from the cast huge wavering black shadows on the ceiling and walls of the lean-to. The door to the inside of the house was at the top of three steps. It was painted white, a splash of light in the starkness of the room.There was a small chest, a chair and a bed against one wall. Two small white feathers were stuck in a crack in the wall. They stood out against the wood, which was as weathered inside as it was outside.

Morning Blossom worked for the Bunkers who called her Doris Tom. Once a day she swept fine desert dust from the floors in the store and the house. Every month, on hands and knees, she scrubbed the same floors with a stiff bristle brush rinsed repeatedly in a wooden bucket of water she dragged behind her as she worked. She also kept the small garden at the rear of the house weed-free and irrigated, and she washed the family's soiled clothes in a large metal tub set up over a small fire pit to keep the water hot. The harsh, homemade lye soap that she used made her hands raw, cracked and sore. Doris Tom did all the things for the Bunkers that pioneer women normally did for their families.

It was not unusual for Mormons to take in Indian women and children. They did it to save the souls of the Southern Paiutes. Mormons had taken the Southern Paiute lands on which they built farms, ranches and towns, but they believed they had been called by God to give instruction to the Indians that stealing was wrong. Most Southern Paiutes did not understand the paradox of the teachings and learned to ignore them.

The Mormons believed that all Indians were descendants of the tribes of the ancient world and they called them Lamenites. It was the divined duty of the Mormons to deliver the Lamenites unto God; bring them back to Christianity and make them Mormons. Having one's house clean and scrubbed, and the laundry cleaned by other hands were some of the welcome benefits of soul saving in St. Thomas.

The Bunkers had been saving Doris' soul for three years. She had grown to appreciate all the comforts of St. Thomas and the Bunker household preferring living in the lean-to and eating the regular meals of white man's food, to living in the nomadic desert camps of the People. Some Southern Paiutes also benefited from soul saving.

Doris and Mouse had known one another nearly all their lives, and although their families followed different paths, they belonged to the same band of Southern Paiutes and had seen each other at tribal functions and social gatherings throughout Southern Nevada.

Once, he had stayed two months in a camp where Doris' family lived and had traveled north with that camp to pick hard-shelled pine nuts from beneath aromatic pinon trees. It had been a plentiful fall harvest and both Doris and Mouse remembered that time — cool, crisp autumn days when their hands had been stained dark and sticky with pine tree sap. The camp fires had burned fragrant and hot, and the aroma of roasting pine nuts and wafting smoke filled the dry stands of pinon trees. The time stood out in his memory.

Mouse and Doris had become friends even though she was a reserved girl and did not make friends easily. She had a habit of dipping her head in a shy, graceful manner and looking out at the world with beautiful almond eyes from under luxurious black lashes. It was a compelling look combined with hair was as thick and black as the inside of a deep sleep that drew him like a magnet. Like a willowy mule deer, Doris always appeared ready to bolt and run for safety .

"Are you well?" Doris whispered politely. Even though she had not seen him for weeks, she was not surprised to have Mouse scratching at her door in the middle of the night for she knew the stories of the knife and the pursuit by Sheriff John Currie. Doris sat on the bed and waved at a chair. She held a finger to her lips and nodded at the inside door. Mouse pulled the water gourd from around his neck and placed it in the chair, but continued standing.

"Yes I am well," Mouse said in a low voice. "How is your father?"

"I have not seen him for many months. He lives with others in a camp near a white man's mine at Tonopah."

Mouse nodded and turned casually to survey the room, careful to let the light from the candle play over his back. Doris sucked in her breath at the deep, weeping scar.

"It is nothing," Mouse said, pleased that she had so quickly noticed. "I met a sidewinder in the desert. He was very angry and wished to talk, so we did. We talked of many things; of the blue sky, the sagebrush, the lack of rain. This snake thought there were too many white men in the desert this year. He had very bad eyesight and he asked me if I was a white man. When I told him no, that I was Mouse, the Nuwuvi, he didn't believe me and asked to taste my flesh to see if it was true. The sidewinder licked my flesh and acknowledged that I was a man of the People, but then he said, 'Here is a little gift for you that you can give to the white man,' and he bit me and traded a part of my flesh for his poison. He said I was to pass this poison to the white men living here, where they do not belong."

Doris looked at Mouse without speaking. She no longer believed that the white man did not belong on Southern Paiute land. She believed that the whites had built St. Thomas and other towns, and made the land their own. Now it was the Southern Paiutes who seemed not to belong. She had argued with Mouse before about the land, about the whites. It was a discussion without end, so she changed the subject.

"You broke the window in the store and took this knife?" Doris asked. She pointed to the hilt stuck in Mouse's breechclout.

"Yes, I took it. I took it in trade for part of the land the whites have taken from the Southern Paiutes."

"Sheriff John Currie is very angry," Doris said. "He said you tried to kill him in the desert. He said you tried to get him lost so he would die of thirst in the desert. When that did not work, he said you tried to kill him and he was forced to shoot at you. I thought the sore in your back was from a bullet."

"This stupid white man sheriff could not catch me," Mouse said with a sneer. "I let him follow me until he grew thirsty and tired. He thought that if he could steal the land of the Southern Paiutes, he could surely chase down one man of the People but he found out how wrong he was."

"Sheriff Currie went to the reservation to look for you. He said sooner or later you would come out of the Place of Birth because there was no water there for a stupid renegade redskin. He left here, but he came back. He is expecting you to turn up."

"This is what I needed to know," Mouse said. "That Currie was here. I have come for his horse."

Doris' eyes grew wide and she shifted uncomfortably on the bed. She said, "Currie is staying in the house behind the stable that holds his horse, but they will kill you if you take this horse."

"They will never catch me," Mouse said. I have fought Currie and won. I have fought the Mojave Desert sidewinder and won. I will take this horse and disappear like a ghost and they will never catch me. I have seen these things in the drawings in the Place of Birth."

"You can read the walls?" Doris marveled.

"When the snake gave me his gift, I took a journey with the creator and he showed me how to read and understand these things. In my journey I rode on the back of the horse, so in this place I will also ride on the back of the horse."

"Where will you ride?" Doris asked. "What will you do?"

"I will live in the Place of Birth and be a cactus thorn in the side of the whites, and I will stick and poke and prod until they grow tired of me and maybe then they will leave this place."

"They are never going to leave here," Doris said. "They are too many. This is now their home."

"It is not their home," Mouse hissed. "This is the land of the People."

"Why do you do these things, Mouse?"

"The white man must be made to pay for taking our lands."

"It is too late."

"Never!" Mouse insisted. "The Nuwuvi will fight and take back the land."

"The People will never fight, for there are many things these white men have brought to the Nuwuvi that are good, and the People have forgotten much of the old ways."

"Yes the whites have given us many things that are useful, but they have brought many things that are not good. Look at you. You live in this house of the white man. You wear the clothes of his wife and do the work of his wife. You have become white."

"I am not white, I am Nuwuvi, and I endure," Doris said.

Suddenly there was a shuffle behind the inside door.

"Doris? Doris you okay?" Bunker's sleepy voice called.

"Come with me Morning Blossom," Mouse whispered. "Be my wife and we will become great in the eyes of the Nuwuvi."

"My name is Doris Tom," she replied, knowing her answer spoke volumes.

"Doris what's going on in there?" Bunker called,, knocking loudly on the door. "I hope you're decent 'cause I'm coming in."

Doris' eyes opened wide and she reached for the nearby candle as Mouse dove for the outside door. He crossed the threshold just as the light snuffed out and the inside door opened. Pressing tightly against the thin wall of the lean-to, he heard Bunker's command, "Light a candle Doris."

A moment later Mouse heard the rasp of the match and could see thin yellow lines where the weak light squeezed between the boards of the lean-to.

"Who was you talkin' to?"

"No one," Doris' light voice replied.

"Now don't lie to me Doris. I could hear a man's voice. Who was in here?"

"No one is here. I am alone."

"What's this?" Bunker demanded. "If there was no one here, just what the hell is this?"

The water gourd, Mouse thought. He had left it sitting on the chair and Bunker had found it.

"It was that damn Mouse wasn't it? He was here. Was he trying to steal something? Did he try to get you to steal some money? Something from the store? That damn thief was trying to steal my money, wasn't he?"

"No," Doris replied. "He came to talk."

"Talk? Why in the world would he want to talk to you? To a girl? Was he trying to do things to you? Did he try to get nasty?"

"What's happening?" Mouse heard a woman's voice. It was Bunker's wife.

"That thieving Mouse has been here. He tried stealing the money box and he was going to rape Doris. I better get some help. He can't have gone far."

"Can't it wait till morning?"

"Good Lord woman, we got a renegade injun trying to rob and kill us in our beds and you want to wait till morning?"

"He is not after money!" Doris defended Mouse. "He did not come to steal money. He would not kill you in your bed. It is only the horse."

Mouse cringed. *Doris shut up. Don't talk any more.*

"He only wants a horse. That's all, just a horse," Doris said.

"Damn, I better hurry," Bunker said to his wife. "I better get my bird gun. We'll get him now. He'll never get outta jail. He can rot in that stink hole."

"Wait," Doris cried. "He will not hurt anyone. He is a good man, only fighting for life."

"Calm down Doris," Bunker said. "We're not gonna hurt him. Just catch him and lock him up."

Even in the dim light, Doris could see the eagerness with which Bunker spoke of the chase. The chase and the 12-gauge shotgun he used to hunt game birds in the low hills north of St. Thomas. Her heart was heavy for Mouse who was only one lone Southern Paiute fighting for what he believed in.

Chapter Eleven

From the rear of the Bunker house Mouse slipped quickly into the darkness, flowing from shadow to shadow as quiet as the Muddy River. The night was stark and colorless, a black and white reflection of reality lit softly by a silver sliver of moon. Once away, he raced on silent feet toward the stable and Sheriff John Currie's bay horse knowing the alarm would soon be given.

The weather had begun to change and the light breeze had become something more. A heavy gust peppered Mouse with a light dusting of sand.

Mouse heard a door slam like a rifle shot behind him and he knew the storeowner was on his way to a neighbor's. Bunker was well respected in town, in church. If he asked his neighbors for assistance in tracking a lone Southern Paiute, they would be eager to help. Soon the town would be roused and the men would be after Mouse. He was grateful of the darkness as he ran on sure, steady feet.

The sore on his back ached and Mouse wiped the spot with his left hand. He wrinkled his nose at the sticky pus and being young, wondered how much longer he would be forced to bear the pain of the past.

He had passed four buildings, when off to his right, the stable barn loomed large and black. If Morning Blossom spoke with knowledge, inside was Currie's horse. Mouse's heart pounded heavily; it sounded thunderous in his ears. The danger and excitement were exhilarating.

Mouse slowed to a walk as he approached the high-peaked building. He knew he must be careful. An abrupt sound, a foreign scent in the stillness of the night could upset the horses the same way a bump or a knock awoke sleeping people. Upset horses might awaken the people in the house at the rear of the lot before he had a chance to take the horse.

Softly, under his breath, Mouse began a song that would comfort the animals in the barn. His song told them he was there only to free one animal from the bonds of the white man. Never again would this horse have to go long without water. Mouse would care for this horse; stroke him, feed him, love him. They would be brothers of the desert.

"Remember me," Mouse sang in his song. "I am the comfort you found in the desert. I am your brother. Remember me and be silent." He hoped the animals in the barn would hear the song, understand and remain still.

The horse barn had been built to house ten animals in stalls running the length of the rectangular building. Five stalls were on each side of a narrow alley down the center. Each opened to the inside of the barn, and also to its own small corral outside. There were four horses and three mules housed in the barn.

Mouse crept cautiously inside the shadowy interior and pulled the door closed. The barn was filled with the comfortable odor of dust, horse manure and dry grass hay piled deep in the loft above the stalls. Spilled feed and straw in the alley between the twin rows of stalls made his footsteps silent. One animal snorted, then was quiet. Mouse had been in the barn many times. More than once the stable owner had paid Mouse a coin to muck out the stalls.

It was very dark as Mouse began checking for the bay. He looked first on one side of the alley, then on the other, working his way quickly from front to back. When he had entered the barn, all but one of the inquisitive animals had come to the inside fence of their stalls. They knew a human had entered and humans meant hay and grain, and although Mouse had a strange scent about him, the horses and mules were not overly bothered because they were in their home, safe and secure. In the distance outside the barn, he heard a man yell, spreading the alarm. The men would soon be here to alert Sheriff John Currie. Mouse had to hurry.

Mouse's heart soared when he finally found the bay housed between two mules in the fifth stall he checked. As he approached, the animal nickered softly, a low throaty sound that came from its chest.

"Yes, it is I," Mouse whispered to the horse. "I have come for you." He stroked the horse's long face. The sparse whiskers around the velvet mouth were bristly, stiff and wiry. The horse nickered again filling Mouse with elation because he believed the horse had responded to his song. The horse remembered the water in the desert. This was an omen.

The Southern Paiute knew the tack was kept in one corner of the barn. It nearly impossible to see in the darkness, but by touch, Mouse selected a hackamore from among many bridles hanging on the wall. A hackamore has no bit and the Southern Paiute believed it would be gentler on the horse. He hurried back to the bay and crawled between the thick boards of the stall.

The horse snorted at Mouse's uneasy rush, but stood quietly at his whispered command in English to "stand." The Southern Paiute slipped the bitless bridle over the animal's head but the headstall was too short. Mouse would have to lengthen it. Anxiety and darkness made his fingers clumsy.

Mouse could hear voices. They were much closer. The men were coming down the road toward the stable. In moments they would be at the barn's wide double doors. He knew he had to move faster.

The horse snorted again as Mouse tried to place the adjusted bridle over its ears, then stomped a front foot and shifted his weight back and forth. All this fumbling activity in the dark was making him nervous. The bay pressed Mouse against the boards in the stall and jerked his head with a snort. The bridle dropped to the ground.

"Stand," Mouse whispered. "Stand! Stand! Stop!"

The urgency in Mouse's voice seemed only to excite the horse. He became more agitated and nervous, snorting loudly again, and again, then stomping with one heavy shod front foot. The hoof landed on the cheek strap of the bridle trapping it to the ground. Mouse swore, a white man's habit. As he bent to pick up the hackamore, the inquisitive mule housed in the next stall reached between the boards with a curious muzzle to look for treats or attention.

Mouse could hear the men outside the door; their voices impatient, and bolstered by their numbers, a swagger in their voices.

They too were in a hurry. "LaVere, you wait in the barn," He heard a voice say. "I'll get Currie out of bed."

"Foot," Mouse whispered wildly, pulling on the bay's front forelock. "Foot!" At the second command the horse lifted its hoof and the Southern Paiute picked up the bridle from the dirt floor. As Mouse raised up, he inadvertently pressed the wet, foulness of the oozing sore on his back firmly into the inhaling nose of the snooping mule.

Mules are intelligent with memories as long as the Colorado River. Once this mule had an infected foot that smelled much like the wound on Mouse's back. The animal recalled the scent and the pain it represented.

As the odor invaded the mule's mind, she tried to jerk her head away from the remembered pain and became stuck in the boards of the stall. The trapped animal instantly exploded with all the fury of a savage thunderstorm.

She began pulling and fighting the boards like an enraged bull. A loud, distressed bray broke the quiet calm of the barn like a clap of thunder and every animal in the stable immediately reacted to the panicked sound. Several startled horses neighed and snorted as they raced around their small stalls. One horse ran from the inside stall to the small corral outside. The other mule in the barn began braying in sympathy creating a chaos of fear and sound.

The big bay half reared, slamming Mouse into the face of the mule. She began struggling harder and Mouse ended up on his hands and knees. The horse ran to the far side of the stall.

"Nephi, he's in the barn!" a voice screamed. "Hurry up, get Currie! We got him trapped in the barn!"

"I'm going to the back," another man yelled. "He won't get out that way."

Mouse was down for only a moment before staggering to his feet. His back was on fire, he had lost the bridle and his hands were covered with fresh horse manure. The turmoil among the animals in the barn continued until the mule suddenly turned her head sideways between the boards and easily backed out of the predicament.

"He's in there," Bunker's excited voice said. "I knew if we hurried we'd get him. He's after the horses. Where's Currie?"

"I'm not waiting for Currie. Let's get him our own selves."

With a loud screech, one side of the double doors swung open and a beam of dim light splashed in across the floor. Between the boards of the stall Mouse could see man's silhouette framed by the light of the moon. The intruder was holding something in his arms; a rifle or shotgun. The dim light outside seemed bright compared to the blanketing darkness in the barn.

Mouse reacted without thinking. He had only one chance. The light from the open door allowed him to find the bridle on the floor and he snatched it up with one hand. With the other he quickly slid open the latch that fastened the stall's gate. Then, with quiet words of command and arms outspread to keep the horse contained, he slowly approached the bay. It had backed into a corner with its ears locked back in posture of fear and defiance.

"All right Mouse, we know you're in here. Come on out," the man at the door coaxed loudly.

The words were a mumble to Mouse. With one final gentle step forward, he reached the bay and began a low litany in Southern Paiute that seemed to calm the animal. He rubbed his hands over the horse's face and then slowly slipped the bridle over the top of its head. It snorted, but held, inhaling deeply of its manure stuck to Mouse's hands; hands that quickly clipped the bridle closed under the horse's chin.

"Damn it Mouse, come out of there or I'm gunna have to shoot you."
The man at the door swung his head back and forth as he peered in.
"Tell 'em to bring a lantern," he called out. "It's dark as pitch in here."

Holding firmly onto the reins, Mouse climbed the boards of the
stall and pushed himself onto the back of the tall bay. With a loud
yell, he drove his heels firmly into the sides of horse and the skittish
animal immediately leaped forward slamming open the stall gate.

The man in the doorway took one startled step backward and
tripped. As he fell, he dropped the shotgun he had been cradling
and it discharged, blowing a four-inch hole in the side of the barn,
causing the animals inside to become frantic. They raced around
their stalls neighing or braying in fear and excitement.

When the big bay first jumped from the stall, it was in a controlled
race for freedom. But when the shotgun fired, it not only blew a hole
in the side of the barn, it also blew the sense completely out of the
horse's consciousness. It thundered from the barn in a horrified
scramble with a mind as blind as the darkness from which it came.
Its pounding hooves only narrowly missed the man on the ground.
The horse's ears were straight back and the whites of its eyes were
bright with terror. Mouse was clinging to the animal's mane with
both hands. He clutched the reins in a leather tangle with fingers
and hair. His legs were locked in an unyielding embrace around the
horse's middle. The whites of his eyes flared like beacons from his
dark face.

He had no control; he could only hold on and scream in triumph
as the heavy muscles between his legs bunched and uncoiled in
a heart-thrilling rhythm that carried him from the very grasp of
his pursuers. Mouse heard a startled yell, then nothing but the
hammering thud of the horse's feet on the hard-packed road as
it raced through the town. A second later another shot broke the

stillness of the night and Mouse thought how foolish these men were.

A dark mound appeared in the street and the horse veered sharply to the right, nearly unseating Mouse, who could only grip tighter with straining knees.

The horse ran through the garden of one house, pounding down tall stalks of rustling corn. He cleared a back fence with a graceful leap and galloped past the outhouse of another Mormon home, then it was out across the crusty desert in a mad zig-zag between bristling clumps of sage and creosote.

The air whistled in Mouse's ears. The uncontrolled flight was like a wind on which he flew with the free-wheeling desert vultures that had saved his life. It was the ecstasy he had experienced in the darkness of the other place and life the way he had dreamt. Mouse bent over the neck of the horse and felt the rhythm alter slightly. The horse was beginning to calm down, his mind was slowly returning. Mouse felt as one with the magnificent animal.

The Southern Paiute glanced over his shoulder and in the distance saw the bright halos of lanterns moving around the barn and knew they would soon be after him.

Suddenly, the big bay faltered and the front of the horse's body dipped sharply. It took only a millisecond to occur, but it was long enough for Mouse to think, to know, the horse had stepped into a hole of some kind, *perhaps the home of a ground squirrel*, he inanely thought in the flash of time. Then he felt himself somersaulting through the air, the body of the horse still firmly gripped between his legs. The next second seemed to last forever.

Mouse heard a sharp scream from the horse and actually felt the agonized sound echo and vibrate in the muscles and flesh of the animal between his legs. He saw the dim night spin in a crazy upside down whirl past his eyes, and heard the audible pop of his left arm as the weight of the falling horse came crashing down upon it. The pain rocketed through his body faster than an arrow from a bow, and new stars flashed bright behind his blinking eyes.

Mouse was stunned as he felt the horse roll away and fight to stand. With a grunt and low scream the animal staggered to its feet. Mouse lay spread eagle on the ground, unable to move or even breathe at first.

Finally he caught his breath and as he tried to sit, the pain sliced up his arm through his shoulder as though he had thrust it into a fire. He nearly blacked out, but after a moment, he was able to bear the hurt and he sat up. However, his left arm was useless.

He immediately looked for the horse. It was ten feet away, its head hanging just above the spindly branches of a dry creosote bush. The animal panted heavily as it stood on three trembling legs. Its fourth leg was pulled up under its body and in the darkness Mouse thought it looked strange as though something, a branch maybe, seemed to be jutting from the leg.

He struggled to his feet, ignoring as best he could the screaming agony in his arm. He felt it with his right hand and found where the bone had broken between his shoulder and elbow. Mouse could feel where the ends of the broken bone had moved apart. He shook his head at the pain, trying to clear his mind. He automatically checked his knife and his back trail.

Mouse walked to the injured horse and became sick to his very soul. The right front leg of the animal had been broken like a dry piece of wood. It had snapped between the fetlock and the knee and the jagged pieces of bone stuck out like white spears. The heavy-shod hoof hung from a strap of torn skin, flesh and tendon, as a large puddle of blood pooled below. With each beat of the horse's heart, a spray of blood was added to the pool. It looked black in the night and Mouse could smell its heavy stickiness. The animal must have stepped exactly wrong into the ground squirrel's hole.

Mouse wasted no time. He knew what must be done and he moved quickly, thinking little of what was to come, what was to do. He searched the ground in a widening circle until he found a large, heavy rock that he could heft with his right hand. Hampered with only one arm, he had to kick at the stone to get it free from the desert crust, then he scooped it up.

He stood in front of the horse, hesitating only a moment before swinging his arm like a catapult on a hinge. He brought the rock in a crashing blow onto the white star that lit the broad forehead beneath the tangled forelock of the horse's head. The stone thunked loudly against the skull between the warm brown eyes Mouse could not see, but knew were filled with pain and agony. The animal dropped senseless, rolling onto its left side. Blood spurted from the broken leg in a dark spray that stained the ground like rain. The horse was not dead, merely unconscious.

Mouse pulled his knife from its scabbard and stepped around the black pool. He began to sing a low song, thanking the horse for being, for living and for the mad exhilarating ride that night. He apologized for the waste of the animal's life and with a weighty pull, he cut deeply into the horse's neck, slicing through the dark brown hair and the thick muscle, into the pulsing jugular vein inside. Blood sprayed out in a heavy throbbing stream until several minutes later the horse shuddered, kicked feebly and died.

Mouse stood looking at the dead animal and wondered at all the possibilities of how the events of this night had come to occur. He remembered his dreams and riding across the dark night in ecstasy. He shook his head at his impotence in life and sighed deeply. He felt the drip from the wound on his back and without thinking, he tried to lift his left arm and wipe the spot. His body lit up like lightening and he staggered from the pain. His arm had not moved. It was useless.

The men were at the barn, their lanterns still bright. The night was dark; the stars still twinkled. Things were as they had been. Mouse looked once again at the horse, then turned and started off into the night. He did not check his back trail. He didn't have to. He knew they were coming, and his steps scrunch, scrunched in the sand.

Chapter Twelve

A swirling wind was rustling the dry desert foliage by the time Mouse entered the Valley of Fire miles from the dead horse. Leaves fallen in the haphazard pattern of death stirred in arid eddies. The spindly branches of bladder plants waved like fleshless alien arms in a ghostly dance that reminded Mouse of his dreams of the future; the dreams that had proven nightmarish, false and useless.

The wind carried the scent of change and Mouse was grateful for its hot breath as it stirred the grainy sand at his feet; feet that plodded slowly and laboriously up and down the hills and dunes away from St. Thomas.

A black shadow was gliding slowly over the land. Propelled by the mournful sighs of a growing gale, the darkness swept across the night sky in voluminous ebony clouds that erased the stars and threatened the moon. In the black distance Mouse could see flashes of brilliance igniting the ponderous clouds and imprinting a promise on his eyes gazing skyward; a promise of moisture, a promise of existence. The clouds carried rain and the taste of the rain was in the air. The wind carried the scent of the moisture and it roused the soul of the vast Mojave which knew and recognized the aroma of life.

Every step for Mouse was a step deeper into the pain that wracked his body. His bicep was swollen nearly twice its normal size and the taut skin was agony. On the outer side of his huge arm was a large bump — a sign that the bone under the skin was dangerously out of place, a sign that Mouse desperately needed help. But he would not seek help yet. First he must outsmart and lose the men chasing him. He would not risk leading them to the People who would undoubtedly be made to suffer for his presence.

Mouse fought the pain. He tried to think only of the journey's end, his small alcove and the soft red sand that lined its bottom. He had a plan for hope and life, but first he must escape from the whites led by Sheriff John Currie. He must lead the men until they were standing stupid and dazed at the end of a box canyon, with no idea of what had happened to their elusive quarry.

Over his shoulder Mouse could see only darkness. The heavy clouds obscured what little light was needed to see more than twenty feet. The wind whipped his hair and blasted his body with stinging grains of sand that stuck to the poison that ran from the white-hot center of the throbbing sore on his back.

The Southern Paiute knew the wind and gathering storm would not stop the men, they would come this night. Currie would know the tracks were fresh and hot, and the coming rain would cool and wash away the trail. He would know there was no time to waste, and so with lanterns the whites would try to follow Mouse's trail and chase him until he lay panting and beaten into the ground.

Mouse plodded through the sand and smiled to himself. He would not make it easy for them. He veered sharply left and right to cross any crusty patches of desert he could find so his feet left no mark. As he walked he sang to the wind and asked it to blow and spread the grains of Mother Earth to cover and hide the tracks his feet left in the red sand. He told the wind, a most capricious entity, that the men who chased him were not of the People. They could not talk with the wind and were a threat to the sacredness of life and the ways of the People.

Mouse crested a hill and looked back. At that instant, the wind broke and for the blink of an eye the dust paused. Far in the distance Mouse saw a flicker of light that seemed like a tiny dim star on the ground instead of in the sky. It was a lantern! The men were coming and they were much closer than they should be. *They must be hurrying very fast*, Mouse thought.

In his mindseye, Mouse saw the posse; one man on the ground with a lantern held high above his head, the others on horseback following closely. Their lanterns would cast broad yellow halos for the tracker on the ground to see the imprints and marks left in the sand. Currie knew how to chase down a man.

Mouse decided the men were at least an hour behind, probably more if the wind had covered any trail. With his mind on his pursuers and his heart in the song to the wind, he turned and started down the far side of the hill. Suddenly he tripped and fell face forward down the steep slope. He spun in midair to protect his injured arm and landed on the weeping sore in his back. The momentum of the fall carried him over and he slammed his broken left arm into the ground. The pain was excruciating and Mouse's mind snapped into a black, desolate place where he became lost.

He had no idea how long he lay unconscious. He slowly became aware that he was trapped in the fuzzy darkness inside his head and that he had to get up and move, but it seemed to take a long time. A bolt of lightening flashed against his eyelids and he opened his eyes and found the darkness of the night was only slightly lighter than the black of the unknown place inside his head. The wind had swept the hillside behind the Southern Paiute and made little piles of loose sand around Mouse's body.

He sat up and the pain made him gag. With his right hand he felt the lump on his left arm. It had grown. Mouse thought the bone was very close to tearing through the skin and even the touch of his hand was nauseating, but Mouse knew he had to move.

As he slowly climbed to his feet, his head spun and his consciousness wavered. His place on the trail was lost and he was not sure exactly which way to go in the Place of Birth. The dizziness was overwhelming and he dropped to his knees. For an instant he considered lying back in the sand and letting the wind bury his presence, but that would make it too easy for the posse.

He shook his head and again stood up. After a moment his mind cleared and the pain eased. A flash of white splendor lit the dark underbelly of the billowing mass above and Mouse got his bearings. He knew this hill behind him and the arroyo where he stood. He threaded a trail through a dense stand of screw-bean mesquite and when he emerged from the other side he hurried across a carpet of large stones leaving no footprints. Even the most skilled tracker could not follow where there was no trail.

Mouse had reached a crossroads: a canyon that ran to the right would take him to the area where he had led Currie in circles two weeks before, and turning left across the desert would take him to his cave and his tank where precious water would soothe the dry burn in his throat. The Southern Paiute made his way painfully up the side of the canyon to check his back trail managing to climb a large boulder from which he scanned the distance. He could see nothing but blackness, hear nothing but the scream of the storm, and even the flashes of lightening revealed nothing.

Had he been healthy, he would have laid a false trail completely through the canyon where his tracks would thin and eventually disappear, leaving nothing to chance. But he was not healthy and his strength was waning. He would have to stop soon and rest or he would collapse and the posse would ride down upon him like desert wasps around a pool of water.

A fierce blast of wind rocked him where he stood on the boulder helping him decide what to do, which way to go. This strong wind would hide his trail and provide safe passage. No one could follow a trail buried deep under the sand, and so Mouse slid down the backside of the rock and turned away from the canyon, directly out across the desert toward his cave.

He was very tired and occasionally staggered as he made his way through the Place of Birth. Although the rain had not yet fallen where Mouse walked, the air was heavy and wet. Moisture poured from his body and made dripping, stringy ropes of his black hair. Twice he fell, but he did not lose consciousness. After a short rest he climbed to his feet and continued in a slow stumbling trot that carried him across the desert. As always, he frequently checked his back trail; there was nothing there but the hard blackness that shielded his passing.

A luminescent streak of red burned from the eastern sky when Mouse finally reached the entrance to his canyon. The wind had calmed and the air felt dense, damp. He pulled his sagebrush broom from its hiding place and weakly brushed out his tracks as he entered the canyon. The sand had absorbed the moisture from the air and it was thick, solid, holding the unnatural streaks left by the broom, but Mouse was too sick and weak to care. He believed the coming rain would hide his passing and he would be safe.

As he made his way down the canyon, Mouse felt peace. The sacredness and the familiarity of the Place of Birth, of home, were good. Even the pain in his arm had eased. He felt a renewed glimmer of bright hope for he had made it this far and he would be safe. If the posse hadn't already returned to St. Thomas, Mouse believed they wouldn't last more than one more day. The storm would wash away his tracks and the posse would leave the harsh foreign desert, go home, and he would find help.

Mouse crawled up the side of the canyon to his cave. His knees and his one good hand left deep ruts in the soft soil of the canyon wall. He dragged himself across the ledge and into his alcove where he collapsed, panting heavily. The soft sand on the bottom of the cave stuck to his body, one side of his face and his hair. He felt its softness and he smelled himself inside the cave. He was home and it was good.

Mouse rested in the downy sand and composed himself. As much as he needed the rest, he needed water much worse. His hemp sack lay at the top of his cave and inside were the things he needed to draw the life-saving fluid from the stone tank. Without getting up, he reached up and pulled the rough bag across the sand until it rested just in front of his face.

Using only his right hand, Mouse reached in to take from the bag the items he would need, but just inside the mouth of the sack something brushed his hand and he jerked back. The skin crawled on the back of his neck and his mind was filled with the vision of a Mojave Desert sidewinder that struck, but did not rattle. His heart was pounding and as he was about to grab the bag and fling it from the cave, a four-inch scorpion scurried from its mouth. Once clear of the hemp, the arachnid uncharacteristically stopped in the open not a foot from Mouse's face. Its pincers were held high and its tail was curled in a circle over its shell-plated back. The six sections of the tail were fat, and tiny light brown hairs bristled from each segment. The stinger on the end of the tail was black and sharp as a desert cholla thorn. It looked deadly and painful where it curved out of a ball at the end of the tail. The eight legs of the scorpion were a translucent pale yellow, as were the claws and tail. Dark joints gave it an armored appearance, and its broad back was striped with dark brown.

The scorpion had not stung him even though he had reached in the bag and touched it. For some reason, it had withheld the painful, venomous sting that would have made him very sick. Perhaps this is an omen, Mouse thought. He remembered the scorpion in the other place and decided this small powerful being was carrying a message that perhaps things would turn in Mouse's favor. For this portent of good will, the Southern Paiute decided the creature would live.

Mouse pushed himself up. He thanked it for not stinging, then used a small stick to sweep it out of his home onto the ledge. The scorpion paused for a moment, then turned and ran down the canyon wall.

Because he wanted no more surprises, Mouse poured the contents of his hemp sack on the sand and turned the bag inside out. He replaced the things in the sack, but kept out a tightly woven child-size basket, a long piece of cord and the leather bag in which he made his tea and poultices. He slid down the side of the canyon and made his way to the water tank. It was light out and the heavy grayness of the dense cloud cover muted the red of the rocks.

Mouse sat on the rounded rock at the lip of the tank. To one end of his rope he tied the small Southern Paiute basket. Throwing it down into the water he was able, using one hand and strong white teeth, to draw up a basketful of water from the tank. He gulped it from the basket. Many times he threw the basket into the tank and drew it up to drink the contents. It was pure nectar and Mouse could feel the moisture seep slowly into his stomach; into his chest; into all parts of his body. Again this place had saved his life. With water, it would take more than a broken arm to kill Mouse, the Southern Paiute.

When he had drunk his fill, he filled his leather pouch with water and hung it around his neck next to his knife. He filled the basket one last time and walked back up the canyon carefully cradling the container.

On the ledge, he looked at his back trail and shook his head. It was dangerous to be so obvious, but circumstances dictate actions and he needed rest.

An intense flash of lightening radiated the air in the canyon and an immense crack of thunder rolled across the desert. The sound shook Mouse and the ledge on which he sat. Behind him, a small stone avalanche trickled onto the ledge. Mouse saw the rocks and sand slide down near his fire pit, but the thunder had deadened his ears and he heard nothing. The powerful odor of ozone blotted out the crispness of the sage and creosote and Mouse was overwhelmed by its potency.

Suddenly, it was raining. The water poured from the sky in waterfall sheets. There had been no warning; no pitter-patter of droplets to issue a caution of what was to come, just water. One moment the air was filled with the promise of rain, the next moment the promise was fulfilled tenfold. The cleansing water washed the dust from the foliage and the rocks, and the wetness intensified the red, lavenders and greens of the place. The blush of life in the Place of Birth became a fresh, sparkling promise that made Mouse rejoice, even through his pain. The rain rejuvenated his heart.

Stripping off his single garment, Mouse stood and let the rainwash the dirt and sweat from his body. As he raised his face to the clouds and the cool wetness eased the hurt in his arm and his back, he felt hope. It was a good feeling. that filled his chest with warmth and his head with a belief in tomorrow. He raised his right hand to the sky and the rain coursed from his fingertips, down his arm, body and legs, to his toes refreshing his life.

In the canyon below the ledge, a small stream first trickled, then grew to a gushing swirl. Water had collected in the small gullies running down the sides of the canyon, then raced to join the flood running through the gorge toward the tanks. Mouse believed the flowing water was not enough to fill the deep tanks, but it was enough to add substantially to dwindling levels. Any water was a gift.

Mouse had begun a song that thanked and praised the clouds and the rain, when another bolt of lightening blazed overhead accompanied by an instant reverberating crash of thunder. The flash and the boom were as one and Mouse enjoyed the power of the light and sound. But the roar of the sound went on and on and on, and it took a moment for Mouse to realize that it was not only the thunder. The sound was coming, growing, from behind him. His arm still outstretched to accept the rain, he turned to face the rock wall above the ledge just as a huge wave of frothy pale brown water exploded off the top of the cliff.

His one thought as the massive wave slammed into his chest and picked him up from the ledge as he might have picked up a cornhusk doll, was that the scorpion had been wrong. His luck had not turned.

Chapter Thirteen

The wall of water that carried Mouse from the front of his cave was an accident of the fickle Mojave Desert. For a thousand, thousand years, whenever it had rained, moisture would trickle from smooth rock faces and the hard-baked ground into a steep depression on the crest of the ridge above Mouse's cave. It would accumulate there, then stream two hundred yards to pour from the top of the cliff and over Mouse's ledge into the canyon below. Every storm deepened the depression, grain-of-sand by grain-of-sand, until its course was etched into a deep scar on the ancient face of the Mojave.

During the last heavy storm, rain had washed away several small pebbles upon which rested a pile of smooth red rocks halfway between the start of the depression and the cliff. The large rocks had cascaded into the gully, creating a precarious dam held together by a sprinkle of dust and the same unpredictability by which the Mojave was altered eon to eon.

For several minutes before Mouse thanked the clouds for blessing the desert with moisture, hundreds of gallons of water poured into the natural reservoir behind the unstable dam. Wind whipped the surface of the water and white-capped waves splashed against the parched shore. Pressure built behind the rocks as more and more rain collected. The immense crack of thunder that deafened Mouse, shook the dam and loosened its hold on the sides of the channel. The second thunderclap finished the demolition and the natural barrier instantly crumbled against the pressure of the water and disappeared in a froth of power.

The water left the reservoir as a solid, massive wave, racing toward Mouse with all the fury of the storm in which it was spawned. It crested the lip of the cliff in an unbelievable explosion of power, pulled by the omnipotent tonnage of the earth's gravity. It could have crushed Mouse, pounding him into the ledge like a buzzing fly slapped against a rock, but it did not.

The wave cleared the lip of the ridge and scooped up Mouse, the Southern Paiute, as the mighty Colorado River might scoop up mouse, the quivering rodent, from its broad shore. And like a tiny animal swirling in the muddy eddies of the powerful river, Mouse was carried helplessly toward a terrifying future. The force of the sweeping wave was awesome. Mouse was clutched around his chest in an unyielding grip that held his shoulders and head above the boiling white foam like a bobbing, corked bottle. He slapped once at the water, but it was like slapping one of the vast red monuments of the Place of Birth.

For a heartbeat, the ride down the slope was a wild, exhilarating return to the wondrous escape from the barn on the back of the bay horse. He was carried in the midst of the strength of life and it made his heart soar. Then the wave slammed into the new river boiling at the canyon's bottom and Mouse felt the passionate wrath of the power of creation.

His eyes, ears and mouth filled with wet sand and water as the cascade plummeting down from the cliff pounded him into the froth in the canyon. As the waters melded into one raging torrent, Mouse was scraped, bounced and pushed along the bottom in a tumble of feet, head, butt; feet, head, butt. He held for an instant to the branch of a creosote bush, but the drag of the water was too strong and he was pulled into its foaming madness still holding a handful of fragrant, waxy leaves.

The racing river collided with the granite boulder at the fork in the canyon and Mouse was scrapped across its ragged face. The sharpness tore deep, stinging gouges into his chest and cheek. He tried to grasp the pocked face of the rock, but was too weak with only one hand. Mouse was filled with an unutterable terror as he felt the river roll him across the sandy clearing toward deep tank. With his one arm, he reached out to find something, anything, to stop his momentum, but there was nothing, and he plunged down into the liquid depths of the deep rock cistern.

He automatically began kicking his feet trying to get a purchase. With his right hand he clawed relentlessly at the side of the tank, but there was no foothold, no handhold in the smooth rock. The pounding water kept pushing Mouse under the surface, but it also created a swirling, boiling action that occasionally would lift him up enough to take a gasping breath.

Mouse fought and gasped until he was sure he could go on no longer when the water finally slowed and stopped pushing him under. He continued to struggle against the granite wall, discovering that if he kicked his feet and pushed at the right angle against the side of the tank, he could stay at the surface and breathe. But he was tiring fast.

The water level had risen two feet from the time Mouse fell into the tank, but it was still too far from the top for him to climb out. In a last desperate lunge, Mouse clawed up as far as he could reach with his right hand and felt a thin lip in the rock. He gripped the tiny ledge with his fingertips and clung like a spider.

His body was a blazing mass of tired muscles and torn flesh, but he was alive and he held on. The broken bone in his arm had ripped through the skin and the jagged end of the bone protruded an inch from the raw puncture wound. The hole seeped blood that spread over the muddy water in the tank in a widening murky stain. The fingers in Mouse's hand supported his weight as he hugged the rock. He sighed deeply and rested. He knew he was not long for this world, but while life still beat in his chest, he would fight.

He would hang from the wall as long as his strength and endurance lasted, and when the water level dropped and he could no longer reach the thin lip, he would kick against the rock until his legs turned to mush and would no longer respond. Then he would gasp and pant for breath until he could no longer stay afloat, and beneath he would hold his breath until his lungs were like fire. Death would not claim this Nuwuvi man easily.

The rain stopped as suddenly as it had started. After a time, the raging river pouring into the tank became a stream, then a trickle and finally stopped altogether.

Mouse had been in the water for two hours when his fingers cramped and slipped from the ledge. He kicked against the side of the tank and shook the cramps from his hand. He splashed in the water and was just able to again lock his fingers on the lip. Even if he had two hands, he knew he could never get out.

He began to sing a song to life. His song expressed his thanks and joy for the existence he had shared with the beings of this world. The wind, the sky, the rocks, all things he thanked in his song of life. He remembered the coyote and the turkey vultures. Even the water that had carried him to this place and was going to take his life was part of his song. For there was nothing without water, and though his existence might end, life would go on.

His chant was low and it echoed and bounced off the sides of the tank. It gave him peace to know he would be able to sing this song of life before traveling to the next world.

Mouse abruptly stopped. He cocked his head and moved it as far from the rock wall as he could. He had heard something. His adrenaline surged. Something or someone was outside! He craned his head as far as he could, looking up the shaft of the tank, but could see nothing. He held his breath and listened intently. There was a dull thud and scrape of something metal against rock. A horseshoe!

"Nephi, you got to see this," a voice called out. "There's water here. A whole basin full of it. Come here!"

The voice was coming from the lower clearing. Mouse recognized it from the barn. It was the posse. Somehow they had stumbled on the canyon that led to the lower tank.

He heard another voice, farther away. "There's water in there?"

"Yeah, it's right here! You can't believe this." It was Bunker. Bunker was at the lower tank.

After a few moments Mouse heard the creak of leather and a brush of cloth against rock. Something splashed in the water.

"Well I'll be damned. Look at this stuff. You think this is where that damn injun's been hidin' out?"

"Of course! There's water here. That son of gun has been drinking out of this tank. We better get the others."

"You go. I'm gunna wait here. I need a rest."

The jangle of harness echoed in the clearing as Bunker remounted and rode away.

Mouse's mind raced. To stay in the tank was certain death. To call out, was to live, at least for the moment, but it was to acknowledge that his enemies had bested him. It was a question of honor, as well as life. Was it better to die here and now, or live with the shame and fight another day? After all the battles he had fought to stay alive, was honor more precious than life?

He heard the posse enter the clearing and someone yell, "Where's Currie?

"I don't know," Nephi answered. "Him and Pablo took a side canyon about thirty minutes ago."

"Man that Pablo is some tracker."

"Yeah he's pretty good for a Mex. He's got Ute blood I bet. They hate the Paiutes. Used to steal their kids and sell 'em for slaves. I could never understand how them injuns could hate one another so much. I mean, they're all the same, right?"

"Yeah, they're all devils. Listen, that Pablo may be some tracker but he never found this place. Me and Nephi did. Ain't that right Nephi?"

"You bet it is."

Mouse closed his eyes and pressed his face against the cool stone of the tank. His breath sounded loud in the small chamber. His fingers were beginning to cramp again. His time was growing short and he knew he must make a decision to drown or give himself up. He shook his head slightly and suddenly something splashed in a circle around his head. Mouse jerked and the something in the water closed tightly around his neck cutting off his breath. Terrified, Mouse let go of the rock and put his hand to his throat. There was a rope around his neck!

Suddenly the rope tightened and Mouse was yanked from the water and up and out of the mouth of the tank. The rope pulled him gasping and gagging out onto the sand of the clearing where he writhed on the ground, his eyes pinched closed as he fought to get his head free.

"What the hell was that?" a voice from below said.

"That you Currie? You up there making that racket?"

"Yeah it's me. I think I got me a Mouse," the sheriff said. "Although it looks more like a drowned rat."

"It sounded like water up there. You got another tank up there?"

"Yeah, I got me a tank all right. Mouse's tank."

With one hand Mouse pulled the rope from around his neck and propped himself against one of the boulders that framed the opening to the deep basin. The rope left a heavy mark in his neck.

His naked body looked terrible. The deep gouges in his chest were pale and puckered where the water had leeched the color from his torn flesh. The bone sticking from his arm was white and stark. Blood oozed from the wound and mixed with the water on his body. His arm and left side looked sodden with the viscous red fluid. Mouse stared at the sheriff without speaking.

"I finally got your red butt didn't I," Currie said. He pulled at the rope that had been around Mouse's neck and began winding it into small loops. The other end of the rope was tied tightly to the saddle of the horse the sheriff had been riding. It was a roan that Mouse recognized from the barn. Mouse thought it belonged to the blacksmith.

"Looks like I did you a favor pulling you from that water. Quite a secret you had goin' here. Good ol' Mouse's tank, huh injun?"

Mouse said nothing. He looked into Currie's eyes and knew the white sheriff expected no answer.

"What's going on up there Currie? You got him? You got Mouse?"

"Yeah, I got him. You guys just cool your heels for a bit. I'll send Pablo down to get you."

At the sound of his name, another man climbed down from the small canyon that led up one side of the tank.

"No passe aqui," the man said.

"Don't talk that crap with me," Currie said.

"I say no go here," the man said in broken English. "To get down, we must go back. Go down other arroyo."

He looked at Mouse, indifferent to the wounds on the Southern Paiute's body.

Mouse stared impassively back, determined to show his strength. Yes, this man had Ute blood. It was a small comfort to think it had been another Indian that tracked him.

"I want you to go around and bring those men up here," Currie said.

"We just tell 'em, 'Come this way,' " Pablo said.

"I don't want to 'just tell 'em.' " Currie mimicked."I want you to go down and bring them the hell up here. You got that?"

Pablo looked at Currie for a moment then flicked his eyes to stare thoughtfully at Mouse.

"Ah, si señor," he said. "Si, señor. I will get the others."

Pablo walked away and Mouse heard him mount a horse that had been tied out of sight up the canyon. He rode the animal back into the clearing and stood above the bleeding man. Without a word he threw down the hemp sack that had been in the cave.

A second after the bag hit the ground, its open end rustled and a large scorpion raced out. Its large claws were raised high as it ran for more stable cover. Pablo saw the scorpion and his eyes widened. He looked again at Mouse who ignored him and quietly told the running creature to come back soon. They had not finished their business.

"And don't hurry," Currie said. "There's no rush."

Pablo nodded, his eyes still on Mouse. "Si, señor, you will have plenty of time."

He turned and rode his horse from the clearing leaving Mouse and the sheriff alone.

Chapter Fourteen

The sand in the clearing was wet and smooth where the now-dead river had combed the tiny grains and left them uniformly side by side. There were deep depressions in the wet sand where Currie, Pablo and their horses had walked. Eventually, the sand would dry and the footprints would disappear. There would be no sign of their ever having been there.

It was early. The heat from the day had not arrived and the morning retained a promise. The rain had washed the rocks, the air, and the plants, and their freshness smelled like new life. The storm had passed, leaving in its wake a Mojave Desert unchangingly altered; an eternal place that would last until the next wind blew or the next storm sprinkled forever upon the ground. Then it would be a new place again.

The wren that lived in the canyon sang and its voice was the music of the Place of Birth. This was life as it had been pecked and etched upon the rock walls and Mouse was glad he had not drowned in the depths of the tank; the depths of Mouse's Tank. His heart swelled. Mouse's Tank forever. He looked at the red rocks and the blue sky and revealed in the beauty of life. Mouse wondered if Currie saw the colors, felt their magnificence.

"You killed my horse," Currie said. He had retied his rope on the pommel of the saddle and walked over to squat in front of Mouse.

"The horse was badly injured. He was in pain. It was time for him to pass to a place where he would be whole and free of pain," Mouse said. His voice was a husky whisper. He was very weak. His body was a throbbing mass.

"You stupid fool. If you hadn't taken the horse from the barn he wouldn't have been hurt."

Mouse cocked his head in thought. After a moment he nodded in agreement. What Currie said was true. He listened to the song of canyon wren and the murmur of the men in the clearing below.

"Many years ago the white man came into this land and stole the land of the People," Mouse said. "If the white man had not come into this place and stole this land, I would not have taken the horse. Even by the white man's law it is wrong to take the things of another. I took the horse in exchange for the land. In exchange for that part of the land that lies north of the big meadow."

Currie slapped Mouse hard across the mouth. The Southern Paiute's head snapped to one side with the slap and a thin trickle of new blood ran from his lip that had split with the blow. He did not cry out. He made no sound.

The sheriff's face was red, swollen with anger.

"You son of a bitch, you've been a thorn in my butt for as long as I been here," Currie said. "It's that stupid, asinine type of logic that's gunna be your death. Sure the white man took this land. What the hell good was it to you? Most of it was overgrown or barren desert. Even the damn river bottoms was being wasted."

Mouse's face was gray. A tiny, shrinking spark lit the darkness behind his eyes. But the spark was flickering.

"It was — it IS our land, our home, you have no right here," Mouse said. Anger gave him strength. "Look around you Currie. The blood of Mother Earth that colors the Place of Birth is the blood that flows in the veins of the Nuwuvi. Even as my blood returns now to mingle with the Place of Birth, we are as one with our land."

"You God damn people make me sick," Currie said. "We're doin' you a favor by bein' here. Hell, we give you real clothes, take you people into our homes, teach you about God and how to live. How 'bout that? Huh injun? How 'bout that?"

Mouse said nothing. A glint of sunlight lanced from between two tall spires and warmed a spot on his shoulder. Mouse looked between the spires and saw a swirl of turkey vultures soaring in the endless search for food. A great sadness settled in his chest. Mouse would miss the warm mantle of the sun. He would miss the passionate aroma of the Mojave after a cleansing rain. And he would miss the warm red sand that clung to his feet as he scrunched his way across the ancient face of the Place of Birth. He would miss the sand that stuck between his toes when he walked. Mouse wondered if there was water in the world beyond. Would it taste as sweet as that from Mouse's Tank?

"Mouse's Tank," he said aloud, savoring the sound of the words. This was a very good thing.

Currie pulled his pistol from his holster and tapped the bone protruding from Mouse's arm.

The tap was like a white hot poker thrust not just into Mouse's arm, but into his very being. He writhed in agony in the sand and screamed.

"Good God Currie what the hell was that," Bunker's voice called from below. "You okay?"

"Don't worry about it, we're just havin' a little talk. Just me and Mouse."

Mouse's body was dripping with sweat. His pain eased enough so he could think, but his body burned with the fires of his injuries.

"You know Mouse, you're acting like you're some big injun warrior doin' the fightin' for all your people. Like you're gettin' back at the white man or something," Currie said. His pistol dangled loosely from his right hand. "Like you're gunna drive us outta here. We ain't ever gunna leave and most of you people know it. But there's always one or two that takes a little longer to learn, to understand. This isn't your land anymore. It ours. You can't win. Your people have lost. Hell, most of you are dying already."

"This is the land of the People," Mouse said. "It will always be the land of the People and we will endure."

"Currie? The Mex is here, we're startin' up," Nephi called.

The sheriff did not respond. He moved away from Mouse.

It was very quiet in the clearing. A lizard ran from a tiny recess in the rocks and stopped in the sun to survey the territory. Had Mouse been able, he would have caught the lizard and eaten him for breakfast. But he could not.

Mouse watched Currie and began singing his song to life. His voice was low but it carried on the currents of the Place of Birth and echoed among the rocks. The lizard heard Mouse's song and nodded once. It did not leave. Mouse pulled his knife from the scabbard that had hung from his neck throughout the ordeal and pointed its flashing blade to the sky. The turkey vultures above heard Mouse's song and dipped their wings.

Mouse used his knife to point to all the paths of life in the Place of Birth — east, west, north south — then he pointed it at Currie, the path of death.

The sheriff quickly raised his pistol.

"You shouldn't have done that, Mouse. That's resisting arrest."

Mouse had no time to sing further before the heavy boom of the pistol reverberated through the clearing.

The bullet entered Mouse just below the left nipple on his chest. He felt it punch its way in and the force of the slug lifted him from the sand and slammed his body against the granite rock. There was little additional pain from the shot or from where his head smashed against the stone. He felt the blow as an oppressive force that punched against and then through his chest.

As his body slumped over onto his left side, the broken bone of his arm was thrust into the wet sand, but Mouse did not feel it. A white haze overwhelmed his vision. Slowly the haze darkened at the outer regions, fading to black toward the center. His right foot jerked several times and his right hand quivered around the handle of the knife. He did not drop it even as the life left his body.

A short time later the only witnesses to the shooting, the lizard and turkey vultures floating high over the earth, saw the posse enter the clearing.

"You shot him? You shot the injun?" one of the men said.

"Yeah. He attacked me with that knife," Currie said. "Look, he's still holdin' it. Son of a bitch went crazy."

The men dismounted and stood in semi-circle around the dead Southern Paiute. They nodded and spoke of the heathen savages they were saving in this God forsaken desert. They talked about how there is always one to buck the system.

"Well that's finally over," Currie said. "Let's clear out of here. Get that body loaded on your horse Pablo and let's go."

Pablo dismounted and walked over to study the body.

Mouse would have been pleased to know Pablo grunted and nodded knowingly when he saw the deep indentation in Mouse's back. The sun climbed high in the sky and began drying the sand in the clearing. The lizard scampered away and the turkey vultures soared. A light desert breeze blew and life continued in the Mojave.

From a crack in the granite at the edge of the clearing, a furry mouse wrinkled his nose as he sniffed the warming desert air. He ran out into the sand, then turned and scampered back. His feet left tiny little marks, an easy trail to follow, and every step scrunch, scrunched in the drying sand.

Epilogue

In 1935 the United States government completed Hoover Dam in Black Canyon some fifty miles south of St. Thomas. Ignoring the 120-degree summer heat radiating from canyon walls, workers swarmed over the area like ants for four years, digging here, blasting there and pouring enough concrete to build a highway to New York. The massive dam is considered an engineering marvel. It not only controls the unpredictable Colorado River, it supplies electric power to millions.

The canyon was plugged in 1935 and for two years water poured in behind it. The angry brown and red waters of the Colorado, Virgin and Muddy rivers blended in a swirl of wetness that spread out behind the dam soaking into the arid Mojave Desert in a slow but unstoppable flood. The silt and sand that gave the three rivers a muddy roiled color gently settled in the rising waters, leaving behind a blueness that rivals the sky.

Inch by inch the waters spread in Lake Mead behind the dam until the broad sea was a vast shimmering anomaly on the rugged back of the Mojave. Desert dwellers, at first delighted to find their dens and lairs within lapping distance of so much life, later had to scurry to dig new homes away from the rising fluid.

The residents of St. Thomas watched the water rise. They would drive in rickety trucks and smooth riding cars to cliffs above Boulder Basin, the large natural crater behind the dam, and view the growing lake with a trepidation that deepened with every inch of water. Slowly the basin filled, then the water splashed into Boulder Canyon, the narrow river gorge that separated Boulder Basin from their homes in St. Thomas.

Within a year of the dam's completion, the worst fears of the people of St. Thomas were confirmed and they were forced to pack and move away. Gently, quietly the water rose until on stormy days, white-capped waves splashed on the doorsteps of the small town. The rising waters were immense and clean and eventually washed away the stains and smells. The splashing wetness filled the cells in the small jail, the general store and the stable. Like Atlantis, St. Thomas slipped beneath the waters.

In dry years, when the winter snow pack is scant and thin in the high northern mountains and the Colorado River has only a meager splash to add to Lake Mead, the tall top branches of the trees that once provided summer shade and pleasing music for the Nuwuvi can been seen peeking from the azure water. The branches stretch gaunt and high like the reaching arms of school age Native Americans seeking recognition.

The craggy redness of the Valley of Fire can be seen from the wavy surface of Lake Mead. In early morning, the rising sun ignites the few sheer, jagged peaks visible from the water as they stretch above the sandy foothills to the west. They appear in the midst of fiery creation. A narrow, blacktopped road leads to the Valley of Fire from the shore of the lake and thousands drive in air conditioned smoothness to view the compelling and magnificent landscape.

The Valley of Fire is a Nevada state park. There is a visitors' center with running water and people who speak of the ancient sea that receded and left the many colorful rock formations. A short drive from the center is a wide gravel turnout where visitors are encouraged to stop and experience the flavor of the Valley of Fire and the Mojave Desert.

The turnout stands at the mouth of a narrow canyon with a soft sandy bottom. There is a brick building, which houses men's and women's restrooms, and a large reader board with a display of the petroglyphs carved and etched into the rocks of the canyon. The board says no one knows the meanings of the petroglyphs; they can no longer be read or understood.

There is a well-worn trail in the canyon that meanders a quarter of a mile across sand and rocks. The trail passes through a narrow area beneath a stone ledge on which there is a small red cave with a powdery, sandy bottom. From just the right angle, at just the right time of day, a sharp-eyed person might be able to make out where a fire once reached up with sharp, hot fingers and left a thin black line on the rock.

At the end of the canyon is a deep natural basin called Mouse's Tank that for most of the year contains a level of water.

Thousands of tourists annually walk from the turnout, down the sandy canyon beneath the cave. In some places the sand sucks at their feet and they can see where lizards have left tiny trails in the red grit. Only the adventurous see the cave and fewer notice the dim line that tells of the fire that once burned on the ledge.

In the summer, the tourists feel the heat of the Mojave as it is magnified in the canyon and sweat pours from their bodies to wet and stain their clothes. They marvel at the water in the tank and wonder how anyone could be thirsty enough to drink the brackish, yellowish fluid. They leave paper and cigarette butts to mark their passing.

The observant can hear the voice of the canyon wren that lives in this place, but few will remember the song of the bird when they view the slides and photos of the granite and red boulders that line the canyon.

They will remember the story told in the visitor's center and on a plaque at the mouth of the canyon of a renegade Southern Paiute named Mouse who created havoc in the white settlements that lined the rivers in the Mojave Desert. How this Indian killed, robbed and ran from the law of the day, hiding out in this canyon where there was water. They will remember that this renegade Indian named Mouse was tracked down and killed by a persistent lawman who engaged him a fierce gun battle.

Many tourists will carry these memories as they leave the Valley of Fire and drive northwest onto the part of the Southern Paiute Indian reservation that lies between the park and Interstate 15, the smooth black beeline to Arizona and Utah in the north, or the glitter and glitz of Las Vegas in the south. Before they reach the wide road, they will come to the Moapa Tribal Enterprises Travel Plaza — "CASINO — RESTAURANT — GASOLINE — CRAFTS — CIGARETTES — FIREWORKS."

The reservation store is a contemporary Mouse's Tank for the People. One of the Moapa Band of Southern Paiute's few sources of revenue, thousands of passersby flock to the store to buy cheap cigarettes and fireworks that cannot be purchased elsewhere, and arts and crafts made by various Native American tribes of the Southwest.

The thriving store is a modern testament to the tenacity of the Southern Paiutes, the Nuwuvi. Making the store work and be productive is a struggle, the way the life of the People has always been a struggle in the desert. Inside the store are books that tell true stories of the Native Americans and of their fight for life.

The young Southern Paiutes who work in the store are caught in a strange place between white values, ideals and motivations, and those of the Nuwuvi. But they have learned to live in that place, the same way the People have always learned to live. The young visit with tribal elders and participate in ceremonies that recall the ways of the People.

The People have endured and will continue to endure. And as the sun rises each morning, careful scrutiny will reveal thousands of colorful moths that live and flourish around the Moapa Tribal Enterprises Travel Plaza and everywhere on the Southern Paiute lands in the Mojave Desert.

The End